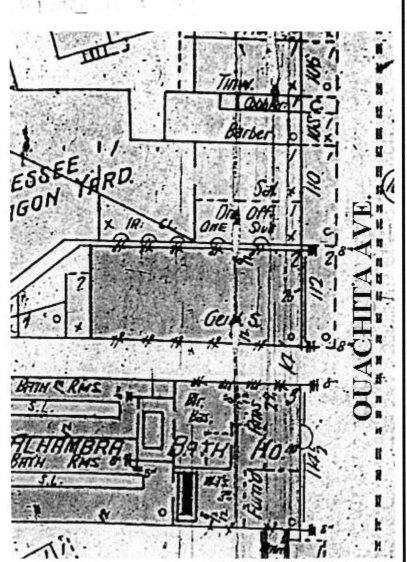

Compliments

Jim K. Randall

Three Strangers Come To Call

By

Janis Kent Percefull
Arkansas Historian and author of *Ouachita Springs Region: A Curiosity of Nature*

Illustrations **by Erin E. Holliday**

Ouachita Springs Region Historical Research Center,
Children's Division
Hot Springs, Arkansas

Published by
Ouachita Springs Region Historical Research Center
Hot Springs, Arkansas 71913

Library of Congress Control Number: 2008933306

Percefull, Janis Kent
Three Strangers Come To Call/ by Janis Kent Percefull:
illustrated by Erin E. Holliday

Summary: Two eleven-year-old cousins, Rachel Lee and Henrietta, encounter three strangers intent on seeing their grandfather, Dr. Robert MacNeil, a Hot Springs physician and Civil War veteran. Each stranger presents their grandfather with a gift: one shocking, another pleasant, and one not wanted at all.

ISBN- 978-0-615-23639-1

1. Historical fiction, mystery. 2. Hot Springs, Arkansas-1895
3. Medical, water-cure. 4. Fashionable Spa. 5. Neighborhood community. 6. Family life.

Printed in the United States of America

University of Minnesota Bindery
Minneapolis, Minnesota, 2008

In memory of my beloved Grandmother Annie Claire Virginia Moore.

Acknowledgments

With a grateful heart, and deep appreciation I thank my Aunt Claire Lee Sims and Liz Robbins, Director, Garland County Historical Society for their input, critique, and encouragement, and a special thank you to Mark Blaeuer, a true friend, who did not hesitate to jump in and assist me at a critical stage in the editing.

Contents

TIME LINE

Selected Historical Events

1818-1876

— Federal government fights for title of Ouachita thermal springs and surrounding area.

1846-1868

— Banking outlawed in Arkansas.

1861-1865

— American Civil War

1872 (September25) - 1873 (March 7, 1873)

— "Great Epizootic." Equine (horse) influenza epidemic that affected 80% to 99% of horses in 33 states, Canada, and Cuba. It devastated the United States economy. Epidemic reached Virginia on November 6, 1872.

1887

— Army and Navy Hospital in Hot Springs, Arkansas opens.

1895

— Hot Springs City Dispensary organized.

— Stephen Crane visits Hot Springs, Arkansas in first week of March.

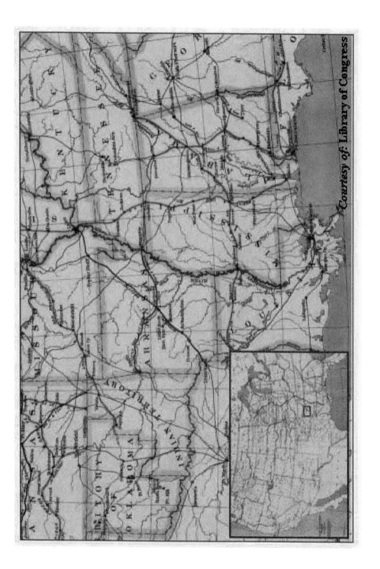

Introduction

The city of Hot Springs, located in central Arkansas, is surrounded by mountains with many hot and cold springs in the area. Much of the land bordering the city belongs to the United States government. While the government land today is called a *National Park*, in 1895 it was referred to as a *Reservation*, because the land was reserved, or set aside, for the use of the federal government.

A hundred years ago and more *health-seekers* traveled from all over the United States to visit these hot and cold springs. Many of them were sick from a disease they called *rheumatism*. This disease made them hurt, but when they soaked in the hot springs they felt much better.

In 1887 the government built a very large military hospital on the government property overlooking the town of Hot Springs. The hospital took care of the soldiers, who had fought in the American Civil War, (1861-1865). This was a war fought between northern and southern states and those in the south called it the War Between the States.

By 1895 Hot Springs had developed into a *fashionable spa* as well as a health resort, because many people, referred to as *pleasure-seeker,* traveled to Hot Springs for fun.

Preface

Dear Reader,

Whether you are 5 or 105 the characters in this story: Rachel Lee, Henrietta, Henry, Jake, and Max—they could have been any one of us, if we had lived in the town of Hot Springs, Arkansas in the spring of 1895.

Therefore, in many ways, this is your story. This was the time and place and these were the events that shaped your young life.

Chapter 1

Meeting the Train

"Hurry up!" Rachel Lee shouted back at her cousin Henrietta. "I can see it pulling in."

Rachel Lee had taken a growing spurt over the past year and was now taller than all the other eleven-year-olds at Quapaw Elementary School including all the boys and her cousin Henrietta.

Henrietta was petite with eyes the color of pewter, a rosy complexion and curly strawberry blond hair that was impossible to tame. Both girls had inherited their fathers' naturally curly hair, but Rachel Lee's was a little less unruly. The taller cousin's hair was chestnut and her eyes were as black as coal—a gift from her mother, as was her darker complexion.

Normally Henrietta wore a big grin to match her sunny disposition that everyone said was like her grandmother MacNeil. But racing her taller cousin all the way down Market Street and across Broadway strained her good humor. "I can't make my legs go any faster," she threw back.

Hot Springs Depot, 1890
Courtesy of Library of Congress

Rachel Lee weighed her desire to reach the depot before the train stopped against concern for her smaller cousin. Concern won out. She slowed down to let Henrietta catch up.

"Next time I am going to wear my roller skates," Henrietta gasped between gulps of air.

Together, they hurried over to the depot in plenty of time to see the passengers file out from the cars.

Train arrivals were grand occasions. The MacNeil cousins took every chance they could to join the station crowd, which was often since they only lived a short distance up the hill.

Many people, most of them pleasure-seekers, had gathered under the depot sign that read, *Hot Springs*. They probably had friends or relatives who had come to join them in a holiday away from home. Of course there were also visitors who came for health as well as pleasure.

An American Passenger Coach
Courtesy of: Library of Congress

Rachel Lee stretched up to every inch of her five feet to see the best way through the crowd. "We got here just in time," she announced as she turned back to see if Henrietta was still with her. Then she continued until she reached an opening on the platform right beside the train. "Look how many people are standing in the aisles waiting to get off."

From long experience they had learned that the pleasure-seekers were the first ones to leave the train. The health-seekers stayed in their seats and waited until the crowd thinned out. There were always many health-seekers on the train that came to Hot Springs to take the baths. The hot water from the mountain made them feel better. It seemed to Rachel Lee that the number of health-seekers increased every day.

"Well, let's keep moving," Henrietta urged. "I don't want to be standing here when they pile off."

Henrietta knew throngs of pleasure-seekers would stampede her if she stood there much longer.

Moving as one, the girls wormed their way through the crowd toward the far end of the platform. "Over there," Rachel Lee pointed to the cargo area.

The girls perched themselves on a couple of barrelheads, the tallest ones they could find. They knew from experience that, as soon as the pleasure-seekers in the first cars got off, they would join their friends and relatives and head out, to the other end of town where all the rich people stayed. Then the health-seekers would make their way off the train.

There was a place for everybody in Hot Springs, but it all depended on how wealthy you were. The girls had learned early that a lot of things depended on how much money you had.

Above the roar of the pleasure-seekers, stage drivers, and baggage men, the girls heard their friend Jake O'Sullivan hawking Mr. Cutter's pleasure-seeker/health-seeker's guide to Hot Springs.

"Get *Cutter's Guide* to Hot Springs only a dime. Get your *Cutter's Illustrated Guide* right here," Jake bellowed.

"Easy pickings," Rachel Lee grinned at her cousin as they watched young nine-year-old Jake peddle his *Cutter's Guide* to the eager newcomers.

Jake was little, but his hat more than made up for his small size. Everything he wore was cut down to fit, from his twelve-year-old brother Henry's hand-me-downs, but his hat was a different story. Their mother did the best she could. She sewed a thick lining around the inner rim of the hat so it would stay on Jake's smaller head, but it sure made him look funny.

"Easy pickings, that's what Henry would say if he were here," Rachel Lee remarked as the girls watched the bulge in Jake's shoulder bag disappear in just a few minutes.

The O'Sullivan brothers had lost their father in a mining accident a year ago. The boys and their mother moved from the mining district, several miles west of Hot Springs to Woodbine Street, two blocks south of Market Street Plaza. Mrs. O'Sullivan was a nurse at the St. Joseph Infirmary on the north end of town. Henry worked upper Central Avenue, about half way up to where his mother worked. He sold papers to the floating population, the people who only came to stay a short time—health-seekers/pleasure-seekers. It was safer for Jake to be closer to home on the south end of town. He didn't sell as many papers, but he made up for it at the depot selling *Cutter's Guide*.

"Hey kids! Only two left, not bad huh?" Jake strutted.

Jake had a funny way of calling everyone in school *kids*. Rachel Lee suspected it was Jake's way of saying, "Hey, we are all in this together...including me." It was a way for him to feel like he belonged. Rachel Lee knew how important that was. Nobody liked to feel left out. She knew even grownups needed to feel like they belonged.

The girls were, as always, delighted at Jake's self-confidence as a salesman. "You're a born salesman," Rachel Lee offered, encouraging his self-confidence.

Pointing to the cars at the end of the train, Jake asked, "Anyone come out yet?" The young salesman had joined the girls at the cargo corner of the depot platform and nestled himself on a nice, soft wool shipment. Mr. Graves, the hide and wool merchant, wouldn't mind, as he cared more about his hides and wool shipping out on time.

"Not yet," Henrietta replied, not taking her eyes off the end cars.

The end cars were the main objects of the girls' visit to the depot. They were the private cars where the really, really, rich people traveled. Most of the time the windows of a car were blocked by curtains, but sometimes, after the rich people left, a servant would open up the car and air it out. That's when the girls could look at all the beautiful things inside like crystal drinking glasses, silver chandeliers, and velvet covered seats. It was a glimpse into a completely different world from theirs.

The town's main street, Central Avenue, cut through the heart of the business district. It ran north and south through a narrow valley, bordered for several blocks by Hot Springs and West Mountains. Pleasure-seekers generally made their way to the north end, called upper Central Avenue, where everything was grand and fancy.

Rachel Lee and her family lived at the south end, called lower Central Avenue. She thought it was silly to call Central Avenue "lower and upper" since the road through town was pretty much the same level.

"Hey," Rachel Lee exclaimed, "look there." Henrietta and Jake followed Rachel Lee's gaze toward the last car, where a man had departed the train. The tall man, dressed in fancy clothes, carried a small, dark wooden writing case. He must have telephoned ahead for a ride because one of the nearby drivers turned down other passengers, and made a point of waving the fancy dressed man toward his carriage.

Jake didn't sell this man a guide to the city because he was not a usual visitor like those who came for health or pleasure;

Courtesy of: Library of Congress

he was a capitalist, a man with really big money, who came to Hot Springs to meet other capitalists. They conducted business, and didn't need a guide for pleasure or health. The trio of children, from long experience, could spot a capitalist from way off.

As the carriage left the station, another much older man, in a wheelchair, supported by two other men, came out from the next to the last car. Before the attendant could place a blanket on the invalid's lap, the children got a look at his empty pants legs tucked out of sight. The children looked on in silence. They had seen these invalids so many times, some in wheelchairs, some on stretchers. Their grandparents' war, the Great War Between the States, which Northerners called the Civil War, had left many men without limbs, and many more just broken in health.

It seemed to Rachel Lee most veterans of the Great War were in pain from a disease called *rheumatism*. Her grandparents had told her that it was quite common with soldiers because of the harsh living conditions they endured during the war, like dampness and cold, bad food, or not enough to eat, and crowded together in unhealthy conditions.

No one had to tell Rachel Lee why it was called a "great war." She knew from a German proverb she had read and memorized from one of her grandfather's books. *Every great war leaves behind three great standing armies—an army of mourners, an army of cripples and an army of thieves.* All three of these great standing armies were still very visible in Rachel Lee's hometown.

The taller of the two helpers pushed the wheelchair to one of the waiting wagons. Most had already filled up and were headed out toward the bathing establishments, hotels, cottages or rooming houses.

The ones who could not afford a ride made their way as best they could. Many times, their family, friends and neighbors got up the money for a one-way ticket to Hot Springs. Some of them arrived in town without a dime to their name. People all over the country really believed the federal government would take care of anyone who couldn't pay for medical help.

"It's so sad," Rachel Lee thought to herself, as she observed a larger than usual group of health-seekers huddled together a few feet away. As if on cue, the kids jumped down from their perches and approached the bewildered visitors.

"Can we help you?" Rachel Lee offered.

A large woman, commanding in appearance spoke for the group. "Yes child," she addressed Rachel Lee with a voice of relief. "We've never been here before, and don't know what we should do. We thought the government men would be here to help us."

Rachel Lee had heard this refrain a thousand times. People all over the country thought the United States government owned Hot Springs. Sometimes, like today, whole families arrived thinking the government would help them.

"Well, it's kind of confusing," Rachel Lee began. She explained the situation as best she could, and then Jake took up the slack.

"Here," Jake announced as he handed the woman his last copy of *Cutter's Guide.*

"Oh, dear," she exclaimed, "I don't think we can go buying any paper."

It's okay," Jake explained, "it's an extra one I had left over." He always saved back one for those in need of help. He and Henry paid for it out of their own pockets. It told about the government's free bathhouse and local charities that handed out leftovers from the dining rooms of the fancier hotels, like the Arlington.

Mostly everyone came for the baths. They healed the sick and made well people feel even better. But poor people needed help with food and shelter while in Hot Springs, because the "water-cure" often took weeks and sometimes even months to take effect.

Rachel Lee also offered assistance to the new arrivals. "As for a place to stay," she instructed, "there are a couple of wagon barns just up the way." She pointed toward Market Street in the general direction of West Mountain. "And two more close by, but I think the ones on Market Street both have room right now," she added.

"Thank you, dear," the commanding woman gratefully acknowledged. "You have all been a great help to us."

While the health-seekers still looked generally distressed, Rachel Lee noticed with a sense of accomplishment that there was a glimmer of relief reflected in the expressions of the newly arrived visitors.

With the excitement over, the kids left the group of health-seekers, who were already absorbed in the *Cutter's Guide.* The girls said good-bye to Jake on the west side of Market Street Plaza. While they headed west back up the hill on Market Street, Jake turned up Ouachita Avenue toward his home on Woodbine Street.

"I guess we'll see some of those poor souls at Mr. Egner's tomorrow," Rachel Lee observed.

Very poor people always ended up renting makeshift rooms above the wagon barns. There were also camp hotels in the wagon yards. They had small rooms, but with more privacy, and cost a little bit more.

Rachel Lee had a thought about the wagon barns. "It's a good thing that four of the town's six wagon barns are within walking distance of the depot," she pondered to herself. "The other two are at this end of town also, but too far away, especially for indigent invalids."

After crossing Ouachita Avenue, the girls raced the rest of the way up Market Street, crossed Quapaw Avenue in five or six leaps, and were soon home.

Home was the "Annie MacNeil Boarding House" at the corner of Market and Prospect Avenues. Prospect Avenue was the last street at the foot of West Mountain. Their grandmother, Annie MacNeil, was usually happy and fun to be around, but you sure didn't want to be late to the supper table. This was encouragement enough for the girls to run.

Chapter 2

Boarding House Reach

Rachel Lee and Henrietta, the youngest seated at the boarding house table, sat on the right side, away from the buffet. When the house was full, and all the boarders well enough to take their supper meal down stairs, the girls would have to eat in the kitchen, which actually pleased them to no end.

This evening there was plenty of room at the table. The head of the table was empty since their grandfather Dr. Robert MacNeil was visiting Cedar Glades, in the mountains west of Hot Springs. Mr. Bartholomew, the French cotton merchant from New Orleans, and Mr. Salmon, the dry goods salesman from Memphis, were also absent from the evening meal. The girls knew these two invalid boarders would not be present, because they had seen their grandmother set aside two trays for them earlier and had already tended to them.

"I wish everyone would just hurry up," Henrietta complained, "I am so hungry."

Miss Amber Hurley quietly entered the dining room, and sat down in her usual seat across from the missing Mr. Salmon and next to Rachel Lee. "Girls," she said, greeting them with a timid nod of her head.

"Hi, Miss Amber," Rachel Lee returned. She couldn't understand why Miss Amber, who was the prettiest woman she knew, was so shy. She wore stylish clothes and was a whiz on the typewriter. She even had her own. Sometimes she could hear Miss Amber typing at night. Everyone in the boarding house knew she brought work home to do on her own time. It didn't seem fair to Rachel Lee that if a person got paid to work so many hours during the day, that they should have to bring work home and not get paid for it.

"How was school today, learn anything new?" Miss Amber asked, glancing briefly at the girls, and then casting a shy look downward, more from habit than nervousness.

Rachel Lee thought she sounded and acted a lot more chipper this evening than usual. Miss Amber always asked what they learned in class. The girls would shrug their shoulders, and then proceed to tell Miss Amber about something that happened at recess or lunch.

Miss Amber Hurley spent her days as secretary for the Mutual Fire and Life Insurance Company. She wasn't an invalid like the other boarders; she rented a room because she liked living at the MacNeil boarding house, and could afford it. She had lived there so long that Rachel Lee and Henrietta thought of her as one of the family.

Mr. Graves, a farmer from Missouri and his wife Emily, appeared for supper and shortened the girls' conversation about their day at school. She and Mr. Graves sat in their usual places across from the girls.

Mr. Graves was in pain all the time because of his rheumatism, but he was doing better since he had started taking the baths. Rachel Lee's grandmother enjoyed having Miss Emily in the house. They were about the same age, and both had grown up in Virginia. Most days while Mr. Graves rested in the afternoon, Miss Emily would join Mrs. MacNeil for a cup of tea, and they would talk while Rachel Lee's grandmother caught up on her needlework.

"Good evening, Miss Hurley. What a lovely dress, and I love that color."

Miss Amber's maroon-colored dress was far too fashionable for Mrs. Graves to wear. But she could appreciate it.

"Why, thank you," Miss Amber replied in surprise, delighted at the compliment. "Good evening to you and Mr. Graves. Are you feeling better today?" she addressed Mr. Graves.

"Very much so," Mr. Graves cheerfully replied. "These waters are like a miracle. When we came here two months ago I could hardly walk, now look. I'm even walking down to the Alhambra for my baths," he added.

In Rachel Lee's opinion, the Alhambra bath house, down on Ouachita Avenue, was the most exotic building in the whole town. Her grandfather said the Moors of North Africa had buildings like the Alhambra, so they called it a Moorish design.

Alhambra Bathhouse
Courtesy of: Hot Springs National Park, Arkansas

Rachel Lee could feel Henrietta squirming impatiently next to her. Grownup talk was not to her liking, especially when she was starving. Rachel Lee knew she was hungry, so was she, but there was nothing she could do about it. From long experience, she knew that Henrietta could become very disagreeable when she was hungry. For Rachel Lee

25

this could result in a flailing elbow to the side. As if assaulting her cousin would bring the food to the table any quicker.

"Well, dear girls, what adventures have you encountered today?" Mr. Graves inquired, turning his attention directly across the table toward Henrietta. That stopped her squirming.

"We saw a real swell-dressed fellow getting off a private car," Henrietta answered politely. "He looked like…"

Before Henrietta could finish her sentence, her father Samuel, entered the dining room, barely making it to the table in time to intercept, and help his mother Annie, who had just rolled through the swinging door from the kitchen with an armful of steaming hot food.

"Hey, pumpkin," he greeted his daughter affectionately with a hug. Samuel was a quiet man with a sad look, who loved his daughter more than anybody else in the world. Henrietta's mother, along with Rachel Lee's parents, had died a long time ago in a typhoid fever epidemic in the village of Cedar Glades.

Annie finished placing supper on the table. Samuel said the prayers and food started around before Henrietta could continue. But Henrietta was too interested in eating to talk, so Rachel Lee continued for her.

"He looked like a capitalist," Rachel Lee blurted out as she placed a small helping of lima beans on her plate.

"Who looked like a capitalist?" Samuel inquired as he ladled gravy on Henrietta's mashed potatoes.

"The man at the depot," Henrietta offered. "He had on a dark green suit and got off the last car," she continued as she simultaneously placed a large amount of mashed potatoes in her mouth, and with her right hand reached across Rachel Lee's plate for a biscuit.

Samuel caught his daughter's right wrist in mid air. "Young lady," Samuel scolded, "that is not acceptable behavior. Where are your manners?"

Henrietta gave a feeble excuse. "I'm so hungry my stomach thinks my throat is cut." That was one of their grandfather's favorite sayings. Everyone laughed when he said it, but no one was laughing now.

"That is no excuse for bad manners. You know better," he chided in a whisper. Henrietta's father rarely had to discipline his daughter, and he hated it when he had to. But where good manners were involved, all the adults in the family were as strict as could be.

The grownups pretended not to notice the commotion at their end of the table, but Rachel Lee knew they were taking it all in. She agreed with her uncle that Henrietta should not have reached across her plate, but still, she wanted to save her cousin any further embarrassment. She knew if she continued with the story it would get the attention off her cousin.

"The man with the green suit was carrying some kind of a fancy writing case," Rachel Lee stated.

"I know the man you're talking about," Miss Amber cheerfully chimed in. She was delighted at the opportunity to help Rachel Lee take attention off Henrietta and save her any further embarrassment. "I saw him late this afternoon."

Rachel Lee thought there was unusual enthusiasm in her voice.

She looked toward Rachel Lee's grandmother. "I was going to tell you about him. He came by the bank today." Miss Amber spoke with authority.

"Which bank?" Annie asked in surprise. She knew this was not payday for Miss Hurley and thought it odd that she would be at a bank.

"Citizens Bank," she replied. "Mr. Leeman's bank... I quit my job at the insurance company and got a job with Mr. Leeman," she proudly blurted out to a surprised audience. "I'm his secretary now. It all happened so suddenly," she stammered. "I was going to tell you this evening...I just didn't have a chance before now."

"I am so delighted for you," Annie gleefully offered.

Everyone congratulated Miss Amber. Rachel Lee was happy for her. Now she wouldn't have to type at night, and Mr. Leeman was a sweetheart. It would be wonderful to work for him.

"Now what about this mysterious man in the green suit?" Annie inquired of her young boarder.

Miss Amber was delighted to continue with what she knew. "The man in the green suit is Mr. McPherson, and he inquired about Dr. MacNeil. Of course, Mr. Leeman told him that Dr. MacNeil was out of town on business, but thought he would return by Saturday evening."

"Did he say what he wanted?" Annie questioned, curious why a capitalist would want to see her husband.

"No he didn't," Miss Amber politely replied. "Only thing he said was that he was from Edinburgh, Scotland, and he had urgent business with Dr. MacNeil. I think he said that he had something for him—like an offer. Isn't that strange?"

"That is strange." Annie couldn't imagine what he would want with her husband.

"I told him that Dr. MacNeil sometimes receives guests on Sunday afternoons," she timidly stated. "I hope that was alright."

"Of course it's alright," Annie assured her. Silently she thought about her husband's father. As a young man, he had emigrated from Edinburgh, Scotland. Aloud she said, "I guess this mystery will have to wait till my husband returns."

Chapter 3

Buttercup's Breakfast

The house was quiet. Rachel Lee lay still, listening hard to the silent house and thought how loud and heavy silence could be. The shadows that filled the bedroom she shared with Henrietta carried the weight of all that silence. That was her thought on silence and shadows.

The girls nicknamed their bedroom the tower room, since the boarding house belfry rested on the roof above them. It was also the highest room in the house, and there was a small door in the middle of the bedroom ceiling, which opened to the belfry. Their bedroom even had its own private staircase leading down to the second floor.

Dr. MacNeil opened the belfry door to ring the bell once a year, on the 4th of July—Independence Day. First, he would pull the cord hard to get the bell going good, and then he let the girls take turns.

As she lay in bed stretching, Rachel Lee knew she was probably the only one awake at this hour. The room was more than a little cold, and caused her to snuggle deeper into the covers. "No sense in putting it off," she told herself. "I guess I had better get up," she silently moaned.

Darkness still enveloped the morning, but enough light streamed through the window from the streetlights below for her to see the stairway. Like most Saturdays, Rachel Lee's day started early, but she didn't mind too much, since she was an early bird anyway.

Quietly she tiptoed through the kitchen and out the back door. Most of the time, because there were people in the house, she and Henrietta had to be dressed before they left their room. But in the early mornings when everyone else was asleep, the girls were allowed to stay dressed in their robes and nightgowns.

Rachel Lee crossed to the far side of the back yard. "Brrr," she stated aloud as she pulled her robe tighter, and wrapped her arms to her chest. She was thankful for the stillness in the early morning air. However, a cold mist had drifted down from the mountains, and she felt it going deep into her bones.

Buttercup, the family dog, bounced toward her at a run. "Just a minute, Buttercup...just a minute," she commanded the dog. Rachel Lee didn't have time for him now. She was at a dead run toward the "privy house." People in the country called them "outhouses," but Rachel Lee thought privy sounded better.

Buttercup was a cream and black lab and spaniel mix. He spent most of his days up on the mountain, as town life did not suit him. But he came down from his wanderings in the early afternoon, about time school was out, and was always there to greet Rachel Lee in the mornings.

"Okay, okay, Buttercup boy," Rachel Lee spoke softly as she and the dog lavished each other with friendly greetings. "Let's get you something to eat," she shivered.

Rachel Lee raced to the back porch, quietly opened the screen door-allowing Buttercup to enter. This was their secret. The porch was off limits to Buttercup and all other animals. Rachel Lee didn't worry; she knew she could lure him off the porch with food.

Buttercup, knowing what awaited him, jubilantly jumped and gently clawed at his young benefactor.

"Just a minute...just a minute....I'm thinking of you, Buttercup....I'm thinking of you....just a minute," Rachel Lee spoke with authority while she scratched his ears. These were Buttercup's code words to stop jumping and clawing at her. "Be patient," Rachel Lee said aloud to her companion.

"*Just a minute* was a good all-purpose command," she thought to herself, as Buttercup, unwilling to let go of her attention, pressed his paws against her side and stretched in delight.

Her grandfather had taught her to use a hand and verbal command at the same time. He said a hand signal reinforced the verbal command. When Rachel Lee used two fingers pointing right at Buttercup, like a sideways V and said, "just a minute...I'm thinking of you...just a minute...just a minute, Buttercup," he would sit at attention and wait.

Most of the time she only had to use the commands twice a day, once at breakfast every day, and on school days she would have to tell him, using her V command, "we'll be back in just a minute. Be a good boy....we'll be back in just a minute." He would sit wagging his tail, as she and Henrietta traipsed off to school.

According to Rachel Lee's grandmother, as soon as the girls were out of sight Buttercup would bound off toward the mountain. As if he could tell time, he would appear on the same spot when they returned home in the afternoon. Rachel Lee knew she had the smartest dog in the whole of Garland County, and that was a bunch of dogs.

Buttercup's breakfast was in its usual place in the icebox. Annie always left a small plate of scraps for him. Rachel Lee also knew that somewhere on the bottom shelf she would find a part of a raw carrot for another of her special friends. Mary, who was Jake and Henry's Aunt, and the MacNeil boardinghouse cook, left the carrot there every Friday afternoon before she went home.

Rachel Lee placed the carrot in her pocket for later and left the porch. Her companion got a whiff of breakfast, and in an instant was on all fours, wagging his tail and circling in delight.

"You're a pistol, Buttercup boy," she lovingly announced. They both went through the porch door at the same time, and as Rachel Lee jumped down the stairs, two at a time, Buttercup was hot on her heels. He leaped for joy as she crossed over to his feeding container by the wood box.

"Good boy," Rachel Lee praised her dog and stroked his head. While the dog ate his breakfast Rachel Lee retrieved an armload of kindling and firewood. Every morning it was her job to get the fire started in the kitchen stove.

As she unloaded her wood by the stove, Rachel Lee could hear the first bird chirp of the morning. This was the official sign of first dawn, even though it would be a few minutes before it was good daylight.

The worst part of her morning chores was cleaning out the extra stove ashes. If she were not careful, she could make a real mess. Rachel Lee left some of the ashes as her grandmother had taught her to do. Then she crumpled up some newspaper, broke some of the kindling into smaller pieces, and placed them on top of the newspaper.

"Ouch!" Rachel Lee gave out a low guttural whisper. Getting a splinter in her hand was one of the hazards of her early morning chore. She finished putting the kindling on and then lit the paper. The slivers of wood caught fire. Rachel Lee could now see to pull the splinter out.

"Well, I can't complain to anyone," Rachel Lee scolded herself. And could hear her grandmother ask, "Were you wearing your gloves?"

Slowly she placed one and then another small piece of wood into the belly of the stove. When it started burning bright, she closed the stove door, grabbed the water bucket, and then crossed over to the water pump at the kitchen sink before proceeding with the last part of her morning duty.

While pumping the handle, she looked out the kitchen window and watched Buttercup disappear in the morning mist. When water in the bucket reached the half-way mark, she carried it over to the stove, and poured the water into its reservoir.

"There, that's done," Rachel Lee announced to the kitchen stove after several trips back and forth from the water pump.

Later after breakfast was cooked, Mary would add more wood, open the damper to the reservoir, and let the hot air from the stove move under the water to heat.

For now, Rachel Lee's part in this everyday ritual was over. She opened the stove door, squatted down in front of the hot blazing fire, and enjoyed its warmth. The heat felt good to her on this cold March morning of 1895.

She would love to have lingered by the fire a little longer like she did most mornings, but Saturday was market day, the most exciting day of the week, and Rachel Lee never wanted to miss a minute of it.

❧❧❧❧❧❧❧❧❧❧❧❧❧❧❧

Chapter 4

Dawn in the Kitchen

Henrietta was still asleep, but not for long. "Henrietta, wake up," Rachel Lee urged. "It's getting light outside, get up."

"I'm awake," Henrietta grumbled as she yawned and stretched.

While Henrietta visited the privy house, Rachel Lee dressed. She had a few minutes to spare before she and Henrietta had to go downstairs, so she perched herself in one of her favorite places, the window seat, facing down toward Market Street Plaza. She could see almost the whole triangle area.

Several local farmers had already lined their wagons along Market Street between the streetcar lines on Central and Ouachita Avenues. A couple of teams stood at the circular-watering trough centered in the middle of the plaza.

"It's going to be a busy market day," Rachel Lee commented aloud more to herself than to her cousin who had returned. She didn't expect Henrietta to reply, and turned back toward the scene below. As she watched the activity unfolding down in the plaza, she silently mused to herself on her grandfather's wisdom about human behavior. He would say, "it's a sure bet, when a number of wagons roll into town early, it's going to be a busy day for all."

Henrietta dressed, as Rachel Lee lingered in the window seat watching the morning break across her beloved Hot Springs. There was no place like it in the whole world. As her grandmother always said, "It's the only place I know of that you can sit on your own front porch and see the world pass by." Rachel Lee knew her grandmother was not exaggerating, because the healing waters of Hot Springs, Arkansas, were famous the whole world over.

"Let's go," Henrietta spoke in a loud impatient whisper, "I'm freezing. Sure hope the fire is going good," she added, and then raced from the room.

The girls made their way downstairs and toward the kitchen at the other end of the house, cutting through the parlor. A picture of her grandfather, young and dark-bearded, rested in its usual place on the left hand side of the mantle.

Most mornings Rachel Lee didn't take notice of it, but when her grandfather was away she missed him.

On entering the kitchen, Rachel Lee added wood to the stove, and the girls huddled by the fire, entranced by the fiery glow. A few minutes later their grandmother joined them.

Silver threads had long streaked Annie's dark brown hair, and now solid gray around her temples softened the lines etched around her eyes and lips.

"Good morning, girls," Annie cheerfully announced, with arms outstretched.

She welcomed the opportunity to draw her two granddaughters close, and huddle with them for a moment by the open door of the stove. "The years pass quickly," she thought. "Sooner than she liked, her granddaughters would no longer be girls but young women."

The girls also enjoyed their grandmother's warm embrace. She and their grandfather were like the mountains, a little worn with time, but as strong and solid as the bedrock of the Ouachitas.

"Good morning," Rachel chirped back, dropping her morning whisper. Their grandmother's appearance was their cue they could talk aloud and not whisper. Henrietta didn't answer, as she was not a morning person like Rachel Lee and their grandmother. Usually she hardly said two words to anyone until way after breakfast.

Rachel Lee melted into her grandmother's warm embrace—soft and full of strength. No one else but the family ever saw her grandmother like this. Her hair was down around her shoulders, and without a corset strapped around her middle her whole body took on a softer, more natural look.

The trio knew the house would soon awaken, and as if on cue Henrietta mumbled, "I'll go," as she headed to the root cellar off from the kitchen to get potatoes. One of their Saturday morning chores was to prepare the breakfast potatoes.

Annie believed in having potatoes at every meal. She believed they were especially good for the boarders under her medical care.

Many of the invalids who came to Hot Springs needed to gain weight, and get their strength back. Potatoes at every meal helped them gain the weight they needed, and it helped strengthen them. The cousins especially liked the way Mary fried them in small pieces with bacon drippings for breakfast.

Annie ground the coffee beans while the girls washed the potatoes.

Rachel Lee had asked her grandmother once why everyone called them coffee beans, when they were really berries. It was a question she asked more to show off her newfound knowledge than any interest in an answer. Her grandmother didn't know why. Rachel Lee then asked all the other adults in her life, including Miss Andrews, her teacher, and no one had an answer. It was one of those questions she stored away and promised herself to find out someday. Meanwhile, it was fun to ask adults a question she knew they didn't have an answer to.

But she did have a thought on why coffee berries were called coffee beans and shared this thought with her grandmother. "I guess it's because they look and feel like a dried bean," she offered. Her grandmother agreed that her explanation was as good a reason as any.

Like clockwork Mary appeared at the back porch. "Ooo, tis a wee bit chilly out there," she shivered on entering. "How me girls this mornin?" she puffed. Mary's labored breathing was very noticeable this morning. The cold affected her that way. Also, her impressive size presented Mary with a challenge on her walk up the hill to the MacNeil boarding house; a challenge, which she met every day but Sunday, rain or shine.

"Okay," they responded—up to their elbows in clean potatoes.

Mary McNulty was a widow who arrived from Ireland soon after Jake and Henry's father died in a mine accident a year ago. John Henry O'Sullivan had been her little brother, and she had watched over him when he was young, now she helped to watch over his boys.

Mary turned to Annie, "I can already be tellin tis goin to be a busy one," she announced.

Since Mary lived down on Woodbine Street, and had to pass by Market Street Plaza on her way to work, she too could tell by the number of wagons in the plaza that it was going to be a busy day at the market.

"Well," Annie stated, "we better get cracking." The coffee had started to boil. "Mary," she added, "I don't think Mr. Bartholomew is up to bacon and eggs this morning. Let's just fix him some oats."

"Surely will. Be me pleasure," Mary agreed. "We have a wee little leftover roast. You want me to make him some beef and barley soup for his noon meal?" she added as a suggestion.

"That's a good idea, it should set well on his stomach," Annie agreed. "And add some chopped carrots if we have any left," she recommended. "It will add a little color and do him some good."

At the mention of carrots, Rachel Lee looked over at Mary who looked back at her and winked, "I think we still have a couple left," she responded.

Rachel Lee silently sighed in relief. She sure didn't want to give up the carrot she held in her pocket for her special friend.

"I don't know what I would do without you," Mrs. MacNeil spoke affectionately to Mary.

"Poorly, Miss Annie, very poorly," Mary smiled in her cheery way.

Rachel Lee's job was to time the coffee. After it boiled a proper amount of time, she would set the pot over to the left end of the stove where the fire wasn't as hot.

While Mary mixed the biscuit batter the girls cut the potatoes into small pieces.

Annie's renters began to stir. Soon her boarding house, as it did every morning, resembled a beehive—swarming with activity.

Chapter 5

Mr. Egner's Wagon Yard

"Girls, are you ready?" Annie stood patiently by the front door. In one hand, she clutched a medicine case, and in the other a medical bag. When Dr. MacNeil was out of town, Annie took over his duties as best she could.

"We're ready," Rachel Lee announced.

Together Mrs. MacNeil and her granddaughters headed down Market Street toward Mr. Egner's Wagon yard. "We're going to have to hurry, girls," Annie spoke a little anxious. "I'm afraid there's going to be a lot to do today."

The beat of the blacksmith hammers produced a wave of sound that drifted up the street toward the MacNeil boarding house. Hot Springs supported twenty blacksmith shops, with three concentrated in the second block of Market Street.

"Sounds like its busy already," Annie commented as she and the girls walked briskly down the street. "I sure hope no one has a serious medical condition, but if necessary we'll send for help."

Annie continued thinking aloud as she naturally picked up speed heading downhill. As a means to keep up with their grandmother the girls began to skip. "It's a good thing the Hot Springs Medical Society decided to open a free dispensary for the invalid poor last month. Poor souls," she said. "Ever since the federal government built that hospital uptown on the "Reservation," in '87, people all over the country have had the idea that the government would take care of them."

"Why doesn't the government help?" Rachel Lee inquired of her grandmother.

"I don't know honey, I just don't know, it's just the way it is," she sighed. "Tell you what though," she announced half seriously. "Let me be queen for a year and I'll get 'em straightened out."

This was their grandmother's answer to a bunch of important questions that didn't seem to have any other answer. Rachel Lee didn't know how her grandmother could become a queen, but she had no doubt that if she were queen, she would be a good one.

Mr. Egner's wagon yard was less than two blocks from the MacNeil boarding house and half way to Market Street Plaza. There was also the "Tennessee Wagon Yard" a short distance from Mr. Egner's.

Most Saturdays all the wagon yards were full of people from the surrounding countryside. Farmers came to town on Saturdays for many reasons, some had produce or livestock to sell, and at times they needed blacksmith or wheelwright work done.

As the MacNeils passed by Mr. Farrell's livery stables across from Egner's Wagon Yard, Henrietta pointed down toward Market Street Plaza. "Here comes the bath wagon," she declared.

"Oh my, they're a little bit early, Annie exclaimed. "I certainly hope Mary has Mr. Bartholomew ready, he's really not strong enough to walk to the bathhouse yet."

The bath wagon was soon close enough for Annie to see the driver. She didn't recognize him and she thought she knew all the drivers.

Rachel Lee and Henrietta waved a greeting to the wagon driver as he passed by. They had gotten to know all the wagon drivers from their visits to the depot, even the new ones.

"Morning, girls," the young driver responded with a wave of his hat and a nod of respect to their grandmother.

"He'll wait for Mr. Bartholomew," Rachel Lee stated with assurance.

"And pray tell," she exclaimed, surprised by Rachel Lee's statement, " how do you know this?"

"Oh, that's Dan Triffet," Henrietta offered, "he's funny."

"And you know him, too?" she asked. Annie was a little alarmed that her girls would be familiar with someone who was a stranger to her.

"Sure, we met him down at the depot," Henrietta responded before Rachel Lee could answer. "He's Mr. Jordan's nephew from Missouri," she added.

Mr. Jordan was the regular driver.

"Goodness me, I'm going to have to get out more," Annie declared good-naturedly. "I guess Mr. Jordan decided to retire," she speculated.

"That's what Mr. Dan said," Rachel Lee answered.

Mrs. MacNeil was strict about when the girls could visit the train depot, and didn't worry too much about them since Mr. Spencer, the railroad inspector, was a good friend of the family, and he made sure the depot workers kept an eye on them.

"Besides," she thought, "as long as the girls stay together and didn't wander off they would be safe." Annie also knew that even though Hot Springs, as a national health resort, was often crowded with a "floating" or temporary population, it remained a friendly and healthy place to live.

"Another good morning," Mr. Egner greeted the MacNeils.

Rachel Lee couldn't remember a time when Mr. Egner didn't think it was a good morning. He always greeted each day as if it were special, but there were times he could be grumpy. Her grandmother said it was because sometimes his shoulder gave him a lot of pain.

"Yes it is," Annie smiled in reply to Mr. Egner who was re-shoeing a team of horses. "Dr. MacNeil is still in Cedar Glades with Mr. Worthington," she announced, holding up her medical bag.

"We will do the best we can," Mr. Egner assured her.

Tennesse Wagon Yard -1888
Courtesy of: Library of Congress, Map Division

Rachel Lee liked the way Mr. Egner took charge and was calm in any situation. It was a good thing, since Mr. Egner had a lot going on at his wagon yard. There were the visitors; most of them health-seekers, who rented out space in his barn and in the camp hotel beside the barn. He also looked after some visitors, many of them health-seekers, who could not afford to pay for a place to stay, food, or for medical treatment. They were the visitors who bathed at the Government Free Bathhouse.

And he had a place set up in his barn for her grandfather's Saturday patients. As long as Rachel Lee could remember, every Saturday her grandfather would see patients on market day at Mr. Egner's wagon barn. Unless he was in Cedar Glades, and then her grandmother would take his place.

Dr. MacNeil had graduated from the University of Louisiana medical school in 1861, before the war, but

Annie had learned medicine tending to the soldiers during the war. That is also where Annie and Dr. MacNeil had met.

"Girls, make sure I have plenty of boiling water," Annie directed as they entered the barn. Annie crossed over to her makeshift dispensary. One of Mr. Egner's extra wagon covers, placed over some poles, gave the patients privacy. A handful of patients already gathered near the covered poles. The girls heard their muffled voices and one painful moan as they went to see about the water.

Annie tended to the country people from the surrounding area first. This time of year most farm families paid with butter, chicken or eggs. The camp hotel visitors were the next group treated; they could pay a little money. The last patients, the indigent barn people, couldn't pay anything. Most of them arrived in Hot Springs thinking the government would take care of them, but soon found out that the government didn't offer much help besides free baths.

"I'll let you know when it starts to boil," a large older lady at the community barn stove offered.

"Thank you," Henrietta answered in a heartbeat and dashed for the other end of the barn to the sheep pen. Henrietta loved petting the sheep, and did so every chance she got.

"Thank you," Rachel Lee echoed. "I need to place these instruments into the big kettle first." She felt very grown up taking on the responsibility of sanitizing her grandfather's extra medical instruments.

"Don't you worry, I'll keep an eye on them," the kind lady assured her. "Say, didn't I see you and your little sister at the train station yesterday?"

Her question did not come as a surprise to Rachel Lee because she recognized the woman. "Yes, that was us," Rachel Lee answered politely, "but we're cousins." Then she asked, "Where are you from?"

"Cottonwood Falls, Kansas, a little bit west of Emporia," the lady answered proudly.

Rachel Lee knew Kansas was to the north, but had no idea where Cottonwood Falls was. "That's pretty far away."

"My goodness child, you're right about that, but our neighbors got up the money for our train tickets, so my husband could come here for the treatments. He's all crippled up with the rheumatism," she lamented.

It was a familiar story to Rachel Lee; it seemed to her that half the country suffered from rheumatism. She knew it would be a few minutes before the water in the smaller teakettle was hot enough for her grandmother, so she joined her cousin over by the sheep pen.

"Look, Rachel Lee," Henrietta squealed with excitement. "Aren't they cute?"

"They certainly are," Rachel Lee agreed. "Look how big this one is."

Mr. Egner also had a couple of cows penned up, and one of them had a little calf that caught Rachel Lee's attention.

A few minutes later the girls made sure their grandmother had her boiling water and instruments, and then they were free until lunchtime and afternoon chores.

As usual their first stop was the corral. Mr. Egner had teams of horses he rented out, and the girls gave the horses special attention. Each had their favorite horse. Henrietta raced over to play with a two-week-old colt.

Prince was Rachel Lee's favorite—her special friend. He was a fine old buckskin with a dark mane and tail, and Mr. Egner had had him forever. He was also the gentlest horse in the whole world. One time when Rachel Lee was still a toddler her grandmother found her sitting on the ground under Prince. Annie swore to everyone she told the story to, that Prince was protecting her from the other horses that might have stepped on her.

"Good boy," Rachel Lee greeted her old friend with a stroke to his velvety muzzle. No one else was paying attention to Rachel Lee, or so she thought, so she slipped Prince a piece of carrot on the Q. T. She didn't want anyone to see her give Prince a carrot because she knew what her grandmother would say if she found out; *Carrots are for stew, not for animals.*

Chapter 6

Mr. Stephen Crane

Prince stood calm, thoroughly enjoying his carrot and his friend's company.

"Good horse," Rachel Lee spoke softly.

"What's his name?" a voice spoke from behind her.

Rachel Lee about jumped out of her skin. The owner of the voice was a serious looking young man, perched on top of the corral fence. He was casually dressed, had a cough, and looked pale.

"Prin..," she squeaked, and then caught her composure. "Prince," she corrected.

"Fine-looking horse," observed the stranger with deep-set eyes and lips with upturned corners that threatened to turn his whole face into one unexpected smile.

Rachel Lee beamed at the praise for her friend. She agreed, "Yes, he is."

"You live around here?" the visitor inquired.

Rachel Lee stood at Prince's side now, since it wasn't polite to talk to someone with your back turned to them. "Yes," she replied, stroking Prince along his neck. "Yes" was all the stranger was going to get until she knew what he wanted.

"Live here long?" he asked.

"Most of my life," she responded. "We moved here from Cedar Glades when I was real little."

"Where is Cedar Glades?"

"It's in the mining district west of here—in the next county," she answered. Rachel Lee thought the man sure asked a lot of questions.

"What do they mine?" he probed.

"Well, mostly quartz crystals, but there's always someone prospecting for silver and gold," she answered the inquisitive stranger. "There are a lot of crystals, but not much silver and gold."

Rachel Lee delighted in showing the stranger how knowledgeable she was about the region's mining district. After all, it was her birthplace. "Colonel Worthington thinks he's going to find copper around Cedar Glades one of these days," she offered.

"Colonel Worthington?" he responded, his interest piqued.

"He owns a lot of mining property."

"He develops mines," the stranger concluded.

"Yes," she confirmed. "You sure ask a lot of questions."

"Sorry, it's a habit I picked up," he immediately apologized.

Rachel Lee had not intended to sound so critical; after all, she was always asking strangers all kinds of questions.

"I can't help myself, I'm a newspaper man...I ask questions for a living," he said in defense.

"A newspaper man," she exclaimed, excited to talk to a real eastern newspaperman. She knew from his speech he was from back east. Now it was her turn to ask the questions. "Where are you from?"

"I work for a New York paper," he answered and then introduced himself. "My name is Stephen Crane, and my publisher sent me out here to cover the west."

"I'm Rachel Lee," she offered. "You going to write about Hot Springs?" she was eager to know.

"Sure am," he grinned.

There it was. Rachel Lee knew the man would smile eventually. He simply looked like a man who knew a swell secret and was dying to tell someone.

"What are you going to say?" she eagerly inquired.

"Sounds like you would make a good reporter yourself," he speculated. It was Rachel Lee's turn to grin.

"I'm not sure what I am going to say," he stated. "I'll tell you this much, your town is like no place I've ever seen, and it's like every place I've seen. It looks like every town in the United States rolled into one—north, south, east and west."

Rachel Lee had never traveled much, but she knew what the newspaperman meant. "It's because people have always come here from all over," she stated.

"That makes sense; I guess they build structures that look like the ones back home." As he jumped down from the fence rubbing his backside, he self-consciously added, "Not exactly comfortable."

The stranger took a couple of steps in her direction, stretched out his arm, and shook her hand politely. "Well Rachel Lee it's been nice talking with you," he said.

"Me too," she replied.

"Guess I had best get into the dispensary and get in line," he announced, nodding his head in the direction of Mr. Egner's wagon barn.

"Grandmother will fix that cough right up," Rachel Lee spoke confidently.

"Grandmother!" Mr. Crane's eyebrows shot up in surprise.

"Grandmother takes over for Grandfather at the wagon barn dispensary when he is out of town," she eagerly informed her new friend. She could tell he looked disappointed and thought it was because her grandfather was not there to doctor him. "She's real good at doctoring, Grandfather says she does better than he does most of the time," she assured him.

"Oh…it's not that. I need to meet with him for a few minutes to give him something," he stated with pride.

"So you don't need doctoring for that cough?" she asked.

"No," he assured her. "So Dr. MacNeil is your grandfather," he stated more to himself than to his new-found friend.

Rachel Lee didn't know why this stranger wanted to meet with her grandfather, but she was eager for her family to meet the newspaper man from New York. "Grandfather will be back tonight. He'll be real tired, but tomorrow afternoon after church would be a good time to come by," she blurted, and then realized he didn't know where they lived. "Our house is up the street on Prospect Avenue on the right hand corner," she instructed. "Annie MacNeil's Boarding House," she added.

"You don't think I should ask your grandmother?"

"I'll tell her. They won't mind, friends visit Sunday afternoons all the time."

He looked disappointed. "I have to leave on the first train out tomorrow morning," he lamented.

"Oh," Rachel Lee replied, "Well, I guess you better ask Grandmother."

"I appreciate your help, though," he stated and took his leave. He then called out over his shoulder, "If all goes well I'll see you this evening," he declared optimistically.

"See you then," she waved in reply.

Rachel Lee watched Mr. Crane walk back toward the wagon barn. She knew he was real proud of that "something" he was going to give her grandfather. "Since he's a writer," she speculated out loud to Prince, "I'll bet he wrote a story to give to Grandfather. But I wonder why he wants to give it to him," she puzzled.

This was the second man in two days that brought a mystery with him. She couldn't wait until she saw Mr. Crane again. At least she would have the answer to one of the mysteries. "Well, old boy," she announced to Prince as she hugged him, "I guess I will have to wait till lunchtime to see what Grandmother told him." She enjoyed his company for a moment longer and then bid him goodbye. "See you later, Prince, old boy," she crooned as she stroked the bridge of his nose.

Rachel Lee walked over to where Henrietta was engrossed in a game of tag with the young colt. "You ready to …?"

"Let's go," Henrietta eagerly interrupted and raced to the fence. "This horse is wearing me out," she added breathlessly.

"What was that fellow talking to you about?" Henrietta inquired as they headed down the street to Market Street Plaza.

It didn't take Rachel Lee long to relay her encounter with the stranger.

"I don't see why a newspaperman all the way from New York would want to see Grandfather," Henrietta commented after Rachel Lee told her what Mr. Crane had said.

"I don't, either, but he said he had something for him," Rachel Lee offered.

"What?"

"He didn't say."

"Why didn't you ask?" Henrietta spoke with raised eyebrows toward her cousin. She couldn't believe Rachel Lee didn't ask the stranger what he was bringing Grandfather.

"Well," she shot back impatiently, "it wouldn't have been polite, and I don't think he would have told me anyway."

"Oh pooh," Henrietta huffed.

Rachel Lee decided to drop the subject of Mr. Crane, which was just as well. Seemed like whenever

Henrietta disagreed with her, and she had nothing else to say, she would tell her cousin "oh pooh."

"First the fancy man from Scotland and now this fellow from New York—good thing Grandfather is coming back this evening. Looks like he's getting real popular with the visitors," Henrietta observed as she and Rachel Lee headed toward the commotion in Market Street Plaza.

Market Street Plaza
June 1896

Chapter 7

Market Street Plaza

Rachel Lee saw several wagon teams unhitched, and lined up in their usual places facing the middle of Market Street Plaza. Stores surrounding the Plaza welcomed the busy market day business. As the girls joined in the Saturday morning bustle, they took note of the horses enjoying a cool drink around the circular horse trough in the middle of the plaza, their backsides turned to the wagons. Their owners talked of crops and weather patterns in deep serious tones. The more harsh and irritated voices most likely belonged to those discussing politics and religion.

The girls avoided the horse trough, as it was never safe to walk behind a horse; a person could get kicked that way. They headed over to where the Hasse family wagon usually parked.

"Good, they are already here," Rachel Lee exclaimed. "Hey, Max," Rachel Lee waved to Mrs. Haase's nine year old.

Rachel Lee was never supposed to raise her voice, it wasn't lady-like. But with all the clatter of wagon wheels, and the gathering of voices around the horse trough, it was tough to be heard.

"Hello," Max Haase shouted over the noise.

Max, a towhead whose arms and legs were always too long for his clothes, was helping his mother set up their goods. His cheeks, naturally rosy, flushed even more than usual as he exerted himself on his mother's behalf.

The Hasse family ran a dairy at the edge of town. Mr. Hasse and his 16-year-old boy Franklin delivered milk and cream every day. Most likely they were already in town delivering to the restaurants, as Mr. Haase had a contract with at least eleven eating establishments.

Cream and butter were their biggest sellers for restaurants. Their butter press left the outline of a racehorse, which was something pleasure-seekers liked. A pat of butter with the imprint of a racehorse added to the character of the town, since Hot Springs hosted races for the visitors' entertainment from late January until March 31.

The MacNeils, like several of the boarding houses and many of the families in the neighborhood, were regular customers of the Hasse family. On Tuesdays when they delivered the MacNeil order, Mr. Haase would drop Max off so he could walk to school with the girls; the rest of the week they dropped him off at Ouapaw Elementary School.

Rachel Lee felt sorry for Max, because when his father dropped him off at school he was always the first kid to school; but Max had to walk home, and because he lived further away, he was probably the last to get home.

"Can we see Lullie?" the cousins asked Mrs. Haase at once on their approach to the Haase wagon.

"Of course you can," Mrs. Haase beamed. She was proud of her four-month-old baby girl. "But don't wake her. She's a handful when she's awake," she added.

"Isn't she cute?" Rachel Lee whispered, although she didn't know why she was whispering. There was so much noise swirling around Market Street Plaza, "it was enough to wake the dead," Rachel Lee repeated one of her grandmother's favorite phrases.

"Look at her little hands, they are so tiny," Henrietta exclaimed tenderly.

Max finished helping his mother set up their supply of cheese, butter, honey, molasses, and homemade jam by the time Rachel Lee and Henrietta had investigated Lullie.

"Hey, kids!" Jake greeted his friends, almost hidden beneath his usual load of *Cutter's Illustrated Guides.*

"Morning," they collectively cheered.

"Are you ready to make some money?" Jake directed his question to his buddy Max.

"Let me get my bag and I'll be ready," Max answered enthusiastically.

Everyone said the boys were born businessmen. To Rachel Lee's way of thinking, they were in a good place to have a business. In fact, she thought to herself, "Grandfather says that if it hadn't been for the Ouachita springs region with its cold water resorts surrounding the hot springs resort, the whole state of Arkansas would have gone bankrupt years ago."

She had listened to her grandfather discussing the matter with an invalid businessman from Little Rock one afternoon in the family parlor. The businessman from Little Rock didn't exactly agree, but that was okay with her grandfather, since he thought everyone was entitled to their own opinion. She also learned that when her family first arrived in Arkansas in the late 1870s, the Arkansas state banks were less than a decade old. It seems that in 1846, the people of the state got so upset with the bankers who had swindled them that they outlawed banking altogether.

"But a state," her grandfather later explained to her, "just like a country or a family, needs money to keep it running. Trading goods and services have their limits in these modern times," he would add. "What if I went to Mr. Walker the shoemaker for a new pair of boots and told him I didn't have any money, but if someday he ever got sick, I could doctor him?" The girls would giggle, but they knew exactly what he meant.

"So when people come here," her grandfather instructed, "they bring their money to pay for a place to stay, food, medical care, and, for those who can afford it, entertainment."

"And they buy candy, jewelry, stationery, anything a person might want," Rachel Lee had expounded.

"Exactly," her grandfather agreed, and that money benefits Hot Springs people, and in turn Hot Springs people buy goods from other places in the region like Little Rock."

From her point of view, standing in the middle of Market Street Plaza on a busy Saturday morning, Hot Springs was the best place in the world to train for business, medicine, or show business, because the whole town was a great big emporium, hospital, bazaar, and circus, all rolled into one.

This was especially true for this time of year, as March horse racing always brought great crowds of visitors to town. These visitors loved to spend money, which made it the busiest time of the year for the town's merchants.

Rachel Lee had no doubt that Jake and Max were going to have a good day's sale, and knew their bags would be empty in no time.

Jake's mom had created matching carryall bags for both her boys and Max from an old black oiled tarpaulin that had faded to a dull gray, but the material was still waterproof. The bags' sturdy shoulder strap proved essential for a man selling newspapers and guide pamphlets.

Max helped Jake sell his usual *Cutter's Illustrated Guide*, but their best seller was the stack of small pamphlets called *Goodwin's Official Turf Guide*, hidden beneath Jake's regular merchandise. It listed all five regular horse races and visitors could buy one at a number of places.

However, on Saturdays many visitors made a point of buying their *Goodwin's Official Turf Guide* from

Max and Jake. There was a good reason for this. On Saturdays, farm boys would come in with their best horses to compete in extra races after the regular five. Max always had a pretty good idea who would win, and for a small fee would impart this knowledge to the visitors.

The kids didn't know exactly why, but they all agreed that this part of Max and Jake's business venture was best kept among themselves. Rachel Lee was sure it had something to do with what the adults called the town's gambling element.

"We'll be over at Mrs. Kirschbaum's," Rachel told the boys.

"Okay, meet you over by the Deaton wagon," Jake agreed.

With more people in town, that meant the grocery stores, restaurants, and confectionery shops would need extra supplies for their businesses. The Deatons supplied town businesses with pecans and peanuts from their farm. Also, the confectionery shops favored Mrs. Deaton's pralines and peanut brittle.

While Max and Jake helped Mrs. Deaton pack Max's bag with supplies, the girls loaded up over at Mrs. Kirschbaum's.

The Kirschbaums had peach and apple orchards. They dried and candied much of their fruits and sold them year round, but their real moneymaker was Mrs. Kirschbaum's famous special conserve. She had a secret recipe so important that Mr. Leeman let them keep it in his vault at the bank. For a penny apiece the girls carried orders uptown for Mrs. Kirschbaum.

Rachel Lee thought the secret ingredient in Mrs. Kirschbaum's special conserve was watermelon, but no one knew for sure what was in the recipe except Mr. and Mrs. Kirschbaum.

"Now, girls," Mrs. Kirschbaum instructed as the cousins carefully placed carrying poles on their shoulders, "you make sure those boys run interference for you. I wouldn't want to see my fruits and candies rolling all over Central Avenue."

The Kirschbaum's preferred hickory limbs for their carrying poles, because hickory bends well without breaking. They had a downward turn and more so the heavier the ends got. Padding in the middle allowed weight to sit comfortably on the shoulder, and notches on either end safely cradled baskets of goods for market.

"They will...I mean the boys...they always make sure no one bumps into us," Henrietta assured her.

"Okay, then, off with you," she stated.

Rachel Lee and Henrietta carefully walked across to where the boys stood by the Deaton wagon.

"Are we ready kids?" Jake asked in his best *I am in charge voice.*

"Ready," they spoke out in unison.

Jake and Max walked side by side, followed at a safe distance by Rachel Lee and Henrietta. The children headed toward the north end of Market Street Plaza, at the junction of Central and Ouachita

Avenues, where the streetcar lines converged. The group stayed to the sidewalk on the west side, as they would have to avoid the bathers farther up on Bath House Row.

Central Avenue - 1890
Courtesy of: Library of Congress

A streetcar whirred by, clanging, and a bath wagon full of bathers, clipped along in pace, headed for their morning ritual.

The young group loaded down with their bulky goods approached the Plateau Hotel at 736 Central Avenue. It stood as a sentinel to the portal of upper Central Avenue, and once they had rounded the 700 block their course was due north.

"Hot Springs is a funny-shaped town," Rachel Lee thought to herself as she trailed along behind her companions. "With the federal government squeezing in on the center and all around, the town looks like a lopsided bowtie. It's no wonder visitors get confused

Plateau Hotel - 1888
Courtesy of: **Library of Congress**

about the government's role in Hot Springs. The city owns a small strip of property on the west side of the valley, and the government owns the rest of the valley and the surrounding mountains. Also, to make things more confusing to visitors," Rachel Lee silently pondered, "the government used to own all the city property, including her family's property on Market Street and Prospect Avenue. And even though they no longer own the town's property, still they control it. That's why no one in the neighborhood can drill for hot water on their property."

It was a strange way for the government to do, but it didn't matter to Rachel Lee who owned the city. It was still her hometown and that would never change. "And besides," she thought, "you have to love a piece of land to really own it."

In fact, on the whole subject of ownership, Rachel Lee agreed with her grandmother who said, "No one ever really owns anything, the good Lord loans us a few things for a short time," then she would add with a twinkle in her eye, "to see what kind of fools it can make of us."

Chapter 8

The Reservation

In no time Rachel Lee and her friends had crossed Chapel Street and arrived in front of Arkansas National Bank at 428 Central Avenue. Reserve Street sat across the Avenue and marked the beginning of the government property called "The Reservation." She and Henrietta had asked their grandfather once why the government named it a reservation if no Indians lived there.

Central Avenue - 1890
Courtesy of: Library of Congress

He explained that, "the government property was "reserved," or set aside, for the government's use."

That sounded logical to the girls.

So far the foursome had not run into any serious sidewalk traffic, but had decided to stop for a rest. About the time they set their loads down, Jake recognized one of his usual customers coming out of the bank and quickly snatched up his shoulder bag, as he was not one to pass up an opportunity to make a sale.

He struggled to free a bundle of small pamphlets out from under the larger and more bulky *Cutter's Illustrated Guide.*

"Here, I got it," Max offered his friend. Max reached in, retrieved the bundle of *Goodwin's Official Turf Guides*, untied it and handed one back to Jake.

"Go, go," Max ordered in a breathy whisper.

Jake scrambled to intersect his customer, a snappy-dressed gambler from Memphis, Tennessee, who always stayed in Hot Springs during racing season.

Max was hot on his heels. "Good morning, Mr. Baswell," Jake greeted while adjusting his weighty load.

"Good morning, boys," the gambler replied, "have a lineup for me this morning?"

Rachel Lee caught the sparkle of the gambler's diamond stickpin, as the sun streamed down Reserve Street and covered Central Avenue in the warmth of the morning light. She wondered if it was a real diamond, or one of the more common Hot Springs diamonds made from the quartz crystals mined in the area. She bet it was real since it wasn't the first time she had seen Mr. Baswell go into the bank. Also, she reasoned he was there to put money in, which meant he was rich enough for a real diamond stick pin.

"Yes," Jake replied in triumph, "right here."

The two made their usual exchange of paper for coin, and then came the real prize, Max's tip of the day. "So what's your best bet today Max?" Mr. Baswell asked as casually as if he were just making idle conversation.

"Johnny Bean's going to be riding his horse, Saddle Tramp," Max offered with a great deal of earnestness. "He's the best running today. Then there's Pale Moon owned by Jason Hardy, and Bashful...he's Sally Hanson's horse, but her brother Sam is going to race him.

For reasons mysterious to Rachel Lee, Max always gave three tips no more, no less. But he made sure his tips were on horses that ran in different races, so each one of them was the best for their race. He was also careful not to say any particular horse would win, but that a certain horse in each race should run the fastest.

"It's funny what people will pay money for," Rachel Lee silently considered. To her way of thinking, betting on hot tips for horse races seemed like a pretty shaky business to be in. In fact, Mr. Baswell was the only wealthy-looking gambler she knew. A lot of wealthy visitors didn't mind losing money on the horse races, but Rachel Lee knew others gambled more than they could afford to lose.

Henrietta was also watching. She grinned in amusement, as she observed her two friends at work, and then turned to her cousin. "Those two sure have their sales pitch down," she stated in merriment.

"Yeah," Rachel Lee agreed and added, "and it's a good thing their mother doesn't know what they're doing, she would have a cow!"

Both girls self-consciously giggled; aware of the peril they put themselves in as allies in Jake and Max's business conspiracy.

The boys concluded their business transaction and rejoined the girls.

"What are you two laughing at?" Jake asked suspiciously.

Henrietta picked up her burden and answered with a grin, "Your mother."

Jake raised one eyebrow and jerked his head sideways, "My mother!" he exclaimed in surprise.

"Yeah, she would have a cow if she knew you and Max were selling those horse racing forms," Henrietta gleefully responded. As she settled her carrying pole squarely on her right shoulder, she gestured her head toward Max and added, "And yours too."

Max looked worried but not Jake. "They're not going to find out," he assured his business partner, and then shot an accusatory look back at Henrietta as they continued up Central Avenue.

"We're not going to tell," Henrietta exclaimed in self-defense, and looked to Rachel Lee to back her up.

Rachel Lee had already settled her shoulder load and had mentally left her companions. She was absorbed in the sights and sounds of her surroundings when Henrietta elbowed her.

"We wouldn't tell would we?" she pleaded with her cousin.

"Of course not," she assured everyone before transporting herself back to her thoughts.

From the moment they had rounded the Plateau Hotel the town of Hot Springs, as it always did, changed before her eyes from an average community to a world famous health resort and fashionable spa.

This changing character of her hometown never ceased to amaze Rachel Lee. She gazed across Central Avenue and looked straight up at the Army and Navy Hospital, the most imposing structure in the world to Rachel Lee. It towered over the city like a fortress, complete with cannons, and at the same time it was a hospital.

"In fact," she proudly announced to herself, "it was the first general hospital built after the Civil War, not only in Arkansas, but in the whole United States of America."

"The finest hospital in the United States," Rachel Lee repeated, a phrase she had often heard in regards to the government-owned hospital on Hot Springs Mountain, "and the only hospital that is itself a fortress."

"Well, let's get going," Jake urged. "I want to get to the Arlington Hotel corner before everyone goes to take their baths," he stated as he started back up Central Avenue. His eagerness to sell his *Goodwin's Official Turf Guide* caused him to pick up his pace, but as he was the shortest one in the group, it didn't bother anyone.

Rachel Lee continued to study the fortress hospital of the Army and Navy, and its patients, as they resumed their walk north. According to her grandfather, the federal government constructed the Army and Navy Hospital for the benefit of the Civil War veterans. From long talks with him she had learned that many soldiers lost arms and legs, and many others endured harsh and overcrowding conditions of camp life, making them susceptible to rheumatic fever; a disease that caused their joints to swell and hurt.

As they passed by the great fortress, she watched the invalid soldiers trudge up the hill to the government hospital, some aided with canes and others carried in bath wagons. Every one of them was a part of the great army of cripples their grandparents' war had left behind.

Army and Navy Hospital - 1890
Courtesy of Library of Congress

Government Free Bath House ~ 1890 (Center-Top)

Courtesy of Library of Congress

Chapter 9

Bath House Row

"Are you with us?" Jake inquired of the girls as he glanced backward.

"So far, so good," Henrietta responded importantly.

Jake and his companions hurriedly made their way along Central Avenue through the crowd of mostly invalids hobbling slowly, or rolling in wheelchairs toward "Bath House Row" across the street. Attendants assisted others more fortunate. This time in the morning droves of bathers left their hotels, cottages, and rooming houses to gather along "Bath House Row" on the east side of the valley, and wait their turn to bathe.

Rachel Lee looked at the grand and opulent bathhouse mansions across the street while still in deep thought on the suffering humanity around her. She could not help but notice the striking difference in the patrons of the different bathhouses. She took special note of the "Government Free Bathhouse," squeezed in-between two of the mansions, in the middle of "Bath House Row," sitting some distance in the back, where the poorest of the poor sought relief from their ailments. It was two worlds so very different within a few feet of one another.

She knew that the popular name for the times in which she lived was the "Gilded Age", and had once overheard a visitor in Mr. Egner's wagon barn explain that it was, *glitzy opulence walking all around tarnished despair.* "You can sure see it here, and it doesn't seem at all fair," she concluded, still watching the invalids across the avenue.

"Well, hello there," Mr. Crane hailed his greeting in Rachel Lee's direction as he raced across the street and joined the group of kids.

His greeting startled Rachel Lee back into the present, and nearly caused her to run her carrying pole into Jake's back, as he stopped to allow the owner of the greeting to step in front of them. Her view of Mr. Crane was clear as she towered over the boys.

"Hello," she replied, happy and surprised to see the New York newspaperman again.

"This is my cousin Henrietta and my friends, Max and Jake," Rachel Lee introduced politely.

"You're the man we saw a few minutes ago at the corral," Henrietta exclaimed in surprise.

"That's right, glad to meet all of you," he replied. "You know how we newspapermen are, we're everywhere and all over the place," he joked.

"Where you headed?" Rachel Lee inquired, feeling very grown up to have a New York newspaperman personally address her.

"Down to the telegraph office, I have to give my editor something, deadlines, you know," he explained. "Say, let me try this line on you guys," he bubbled with enthusiasm as he pulled out some sheets of paper from his jacket pocket.

The kids listened intently as Stephen Crane read from his article on their hometown. *Crowds swarm to these baths. A man becomes a creature of three conditions. He is about to take a bath—he is taking a bath—he has taken a bath.*

His audience chuckled at his observation.

"You like it?" he asked in earnest.

"It's funny," Jake responded, and the rest agreed.

"Oh, good, see you later," he announced and was gone as quickly as he had appeared.

"Man! We got to get going," Jake declared, and proceeded toward the confectionery shops. The others followed, and they had not gone far before they met up with Jake's brother, Henry, coming down the street from the Arlington Hotel.

"Off to Mrs. Rozzetti's?" he inquired, still standing in the street with his matching carryall bag slung over one shoulder.

"And Mrs. Carver's too," Henrietta happily announced.

"That's why we are carrying so much," Rachel Lee exclaimed.

She and Henrietta, like all the other kids in the neighborhood, looked up to Henry. He was big for his age, like Rachel Lee, and this made him a good protector, but more than that, he was just a swell fellow.

Rachel Lee also thought he was the handsomest-looking boy in the whole town. He had coal black wavy hair under his cap and the prettiest dark blue eyes.

"Yeah, look here," Max offered, holding his carryall open.

Leaning forward, Henry peered in, and whistled. "Ooh!" he exclaimed. "Guess you need to go unload this before you can start selling your papers," he stated matter of factly.

"Guess I'll wait till ya'll get back before I tell you my news," he teased, and headed back to his corner on Fountain Street in front of the Arlington Hotel.

The group started up again, but at a much faster pace. They were keen to know all about Henry's news.

"Wonder what he knows we don't," Jake breathlessly pondered aloud to no one in particular.

"Guess we will find out soon enough," Max breathed hard under the labor of his load.

Five minutes more and they were almost there. It was the one hundred block of Central Avenue and the end of the commercial district. From here Central Avenue split off into two directions: Whittington Avenue on the left and Park Avenue on the right.

"Is everyone okay?" Jake asked.

"Still here," Henrietta answered, happy in the experience of walking along Central Avenue toward the glamorous end of town. Here wealthy pleasure-seekers were on display in their finely upholstered carriages with high-prancing horses, sauntering along the Avenue as patrons of the finer shops.

Central Avenue - 1890
Courtesy of: Library of Congress

Upper Central Avenue for Max, Jake, Rachel Lee and Henrietta, represented a never-ending kaleidoscope of colorful characters, like actors on their own personal stage.

Rachel Lee saw it as beautiful and untouched by the everyday misery encountered elsewhere in her hometown. Both the beauty and the misery were real, and a part of her life, but she could never understand why some people had so much and others so little.

All that she saw made her grateful for her life. She had neither too much nor too little, but just what she could handle. And she knew she was loved just for who she was, and not for what she had. On the other hand, she was grateful her family could provide her with protection from poverty.

Most of all, her life was full of possibilities—a most prized possession to her way of thinking because possibilities meant you had choices, and when you had choices you had freedom. As her grandmother had observed, *the pampered little song bird could not choose to leave its gilded cage and the plain little sparrow, found it was forever imprisoned by hunger.*

Arlington Hotel - 1890

Chapter 10

Henry's Big News

"I got it," Max stated as he held the screen door open while Jake caught the main door to Mrs. Rozzetti's fancy confectionery store.

Like most of the store owners in town, Mrs. Rozzetti worked within the confines of a long narrow shop, lined on either side with glass counters to highlight the merchant's stock.

"Boy, I'm glad to unload this stuff," Henrietta complained as she and Rachel Lee carefully threaded their way through Mrs. Rozzetti's shop door.

"Oh, boy, me too," Rachel Lee agreed. "I feel like this pole has grown to my shoulder."

Mrs. Rozzetti's fancy confectionery shop also differed from most of the shops in town, at least from the shops in Market Street Plaza. It catered to the very wealthiest pleasure-seekers, and her establishment reflected their wealth. Toward the back, an ornate heating stove surrounded by well carved chairs, dominated the interior. Off to the left was Mrs. Rozzetti's rosewood writing table, where she conducted her business, and to the right a door led back to her storeroom.

"It's just us," Jake announced on entering. He didn't want to interrupt Mrs. Rozzetti and her customers, a large well-dressed older woman supported by a cane, accompanied by a much younger and plainly dressed woman.

"Oh, good...good," she answered. "I'll settle up with you in a minute."

As she turned her attention back to her customers, the kids carefully moved to the back, and unloaded all their goods except for two jars of Mrs. Kirschbaum's special conserve, and three bags of Mrs. Deaton's peanut brittle. The girls also left their carrying poles for Mr. Kirschbaum to pick up later in the day.

"Max, hold these while I divide the *Cutter's Guides*," Jake suggested.

While Max held the bundle of *Turf Guides*, and received his share of the pamphlets, the girls peeked around the storeroom door to feast their eyes on all the beautiful furnishings at the back of the store.

After concluding their business with Mrs. Rozzetti, they hurried over to Mrs. Carver's store, a few doors up the street, and then took off at a run for Fountain Street, with the boys way out in the lead.

"Rachel Lee!" Henrietta panted in earnest, "I can't go any faster," she pleaded.

"Go on, we'll catch up," Rachel Lee yelled out in the boys' direction, and then slowed down to a walk.

"Okay," Jake waved.

"Just as well," Rachel Lee stated when Henrietta caught up with her. "Those boys are more interested in selling their racing forms right now than in talking to Henry."

"You're right there," Henrietta agreed, "I don't blame them, it's a good time to sell the forms. Look at the crowd," she exclaimed, pointing toward the bathhouses.

Rachel Lee gazed across and down Central Avenue toward Fountain Street, where Max and Jake had already staked out territory near Henry in front of the Arlington Hotel. "Looks like all three of the boys are having a good day," she observed. "I wish we could sell papers," she lamented, knowing that her grandparents frowned on the idea.

"Me, too," Henrietta agreed. "Think how much money we could make! We could buy anything we wanted," she declared.

"It doesn't make sense to me," Rachel Lee complained, "Here we have six newspapers in town and thousands of customers…I don't see what would be so wrong about selling papers on the street corner like the boys."

"Me, neither, it's not fair," Henrietta echoed. She pondered on the subject for a moment and then added, "I don't see any point in pushing it, though."

Rachel Lee nodded in half-hearted agreement.

Both girls knew there was no use in reasoning with their grandparents, since this was one of those issues that always ended with an "It's just not done" argument from their grandmother.

Rachel Lee and Henrietta walked up to the Arlington Hotel and continued up Fountain Street past the boys. They knew their friends would be busy for the next few minutes, but they didn't want to leave downtown until they had found out what Henry's big news was.

"Let's go up there," Rachel Lee nodded. They headed in the direction of her nod farther up Fountain Street out of everybody's way. It was a good place to hang around until the morning bathers had left the area.

Henry, having kept one eye on the girls, waved the okay sign, and they scrambled down the street to hear his big news.

The cousins could see that Max and Jake had already joined Henry.

"You're not going to believe this!" Henry exclaimed as an opener to his story. "Earlier this morning," he continued, knowing he had his audience's full attention, "I was here in the Arlington lobby delivering my papers when I heard a man asking the concierge about your grandfather."

"What did he look like?" Henrietta asked.

"He was an older man about your grandparents' age," Henry answered, "and he was in a wheelchair. I think he was in the war," Henry looked down with a pained expression and added, "He didn't have any legs."

The kids were silent. They had seen a lot of older men their grandfather's age with missing arms and legs, but mostly they only had one leg, or arm or a hand missing.

"Both legs gone, that's awful," Rachel Lee sadly thought.

"Anyway," Henry continued with his story, "Mr. Johnson knows that I'm from the Market Street Plaza neighborhood, so he knew I could tell the stranger what he wanted to know about your grandfather."

"What did he want to know?" Henrietta again interrupted.

"Well, the stranger knew your grandfather was out of town," Henry patiently continued, "and that he shares an office with Dr. Moore in back of *Taylor/Moore Drug Store* on Ouachita Avenue. But he needed to know when Dr. MacNeil was due back. Said he had something that belonged to him, and he wanted to give it back to him."

"What!" Henrietta dropped her jaw.

"Well, for goodness sakes!" Rachel Lee exclaimed, sounding like her grandmother, "a third gift!"

"That's what I thought," Henry stated. "He didn't say what it was, but he was right pleased with himself when he said it," Henry grinned, showing off a dimple in his right cheek. "I told him people always visit each other around here on Sunday afternoons, and thought it would be alright for him to come to your house about mid-afternoon or later."

"I don't think Grandfather will mind, I think the Scotsman is coming then too," Rachel Lee stated.

"Man," Henry exclaimed, "I can't wait to find out what all these men want with your grandfather." His companions were in total agreement. Henry barely got through with his story before more customers appeared, and the girls had to take their leave.

"Battle stations," Jake rapped out in a loud whisper to Max. "See you kids later," he addressed the girls.

"Later," Max added.

"Bye," the girls both spoke at once.

The boys hurried back to their usual selling place a short distance from Henry.

"Thanks, Henry, we'll let Grandmother know about the wheelchair man," Rachel Lee spoke as she and Henrietta took leave to let Henry go back to work.

"Catch you later," he offered as he turned to a young couple that looked dressed more for a morning drive than a bath.

Chapter 11

Down To the Meat Market

The MacNeil carriage house, situated in one corner of the backyard, was a catch-all building that had everything in it, but a carriage. Like many of their neighbors, they didn't have a need to own private transportation, because the Market Street Plaza community was small and self-contained. Every kind of business and retail store abound within walking distance of the surrounding neighborhoods.

Hot Springs public streetcar lines ran on either side of Market Street Plaza. Also, a person could always rent a horse or carriage from the livery stable if they were going a short distance; or they could catch a train headed to anywhere in the United States, Mexico, or Canada.

"My turn," Rachel Lee exclaimed, and ran over to the middle of the carriage house where the cart was stored.

The girls took turns taking the cart down to Mr. Egner's for pickups. Going downhill with an empty cart didn't present much of a challenge, but coming back home, uphill with the full cart, was a different story.

Rachel Lee reached overhead and took down three large chicken cages, and one small one. Roosters couldn't be put in the same cage, because they would fight each other. Also, it was hard to pick a rooster up, because they attack with their spurs—a long claw on either side of their foot.

In no time the girls appeared with their wagon and chicken cages at Mr. Egner's Wagon Barn.

"Mr. Egner, we're here for the roosters," Rachel Lee called out, wheeling her cart over to the area of the barn where the winged creatures were caged.

"Your timing is good," Mr. Egner exclaimed as he crossed over from his work area to where the girls were stacking their empty cages.

"These critters can sure enough be mean," Mr. Egner commented as he placed the caged roosters in the girls' cart. "Henrietta, that little one is yours, too," he pointed to a lone chick in a small cage.

Henrietta put the cage on top of the rooster cages and retrieved the chick from its holder.

"Thanks, Mr. Egner," Rachel Lee spoke in earnest. No way did she want to pick up a rooster, not even in a cage; it could still peck her. "We'll see you later," Rachel Lee called back as she aimed her cartload of roosters toward the barn door.

"Good-bye," Henrietta offered to Mr. Egner as she trailed behind the cart holding the chick close to her and petting its fussy neck and back.

"Bye now," he returned as he headed back to his work table.

Mr. MacDonald's meat shop was located on the east end of the plaza, at the far end of Market Street. The girls noticed that wagons still filled the plaza, but there were less people now. Mrs. Kirschbaum had joined Mrs. Deaton for lunch at her wagon, and the girls waved to them as they passed.

"You girls take care those roosters don't spur you," Mrs. Deaton warned.

"We will," they promised.

Mr. MacDonald's wife was at the counter when Henrietta walked in.

"Mrs. MacDonald we have three roosters," Henrietta announced.

Well, let's go see," she stated, as she walked out from behind the counter and followed Henrietta back outside where Rachel Lee stood waiting by the cart.

"Hello, Rachel Lee," Mrs. MacDonald greeted.

"Hello, Mrs. MacDonald. "Grandmother asked if you could put the roosters on account, and she needs a chicken to cook for Sunday dinner as usual."

"We can sure do that," Mrs. MacDonald assured her, and took charge of the cart. "Let me take the cart around back to Mr. MacDonald, and I'll get a chicken from the ice chest, and be back in a minute."

"Okay," Rachel Lee agreed as she handed the cart over to Mrs. MacDonald.

The girls sat on the front step of the meat market until Mrs. MacDonald returned with the cart and their grandmother's order.

"There you go!" Mrs. MacDonald announced, handing Rachel Lee a bag. "Tell your grandmother I said hello."

"We will," the girls answered at the same time.

Henrietta placed the chick in its cage in the cart and turned for home. The girls hurried back up Market Street, both anxious to tell their grandfather everything about the three mysterious men who were going to come calling.

Chapter 12

Grandparents Private Quarters

Rachel Lee placed the meat market bag in the icebox, next to some leftovers, and went into the kitchen right behind Henrietta.

"Oh, boy, chocolate pie," Henrietta proclaimed in excitement.

"And butterscotch," Rachel Lee ventured, but she really didn't think that Mary had forgotten her. It was Mary's custom to treat the girls to their favorite pie every now and then.

"Of course, child…can't make one without the other," Mary responded as she continued to place strips of pastry in a crisscross design across the top of a third pie. "And apple pie for your grandfather," she beamed.

"Mary is the best," Rachel Lee thought to herself.

The girls watched Mary prepare their grandfather's favorite pie with the same pride she showed in everything she did. Rachel Lee studied on how she had not known Mary McNulty long, but could not remember what life was like before Mary came into their lives. Like her grandmother, she had a way of quietly filling a room with warmth and laughter, and also like her grandmother, Mary McNulty was strong but gentle at the same time.

Mary placed the pies in the stove and turned to catch Rachel Lee deep in thought. "Land sakes," Mary exclaimed, "ye be the dreamiest child I ever met."

Rachel Lee took that as a compliment and grinned.

"Can we go up to see Grandfather now?" Henrietta pleaded.

"I think it would be alright," Mary assured them, "but be quiet, the sick folk are still resting."

The girls didn't need a second invitation.

They made their way up to their grandparents' private rooms. Quietly they tiptoed past their grandmother, who was dozing and slipped through the partially closed doors that led to a parlor and bath.

 Dr. MacNeil, wrapped in his bathrobe, leaned comfortably in his wicker chair. His gray hair, towel-dried and ruffled, was still damp from his bath. He was a tall man and spilled out from his place of rest.

The girls caught him casually scanning the 1895 edition of the *Taylor/Moore Drug Store* farmer's almanac. Dr. MacNeil's son Samuel and Dr. Moore's son Milton were both keen on the almanac as a way for the drug store to advertise. The town supported over twenty drug, apothecary, and pharmacy stores. The young druggists believed that the almanac would help them stand out.

"Sweet peas," Dr. MacNeil exclaimed in a low voice, using his favorite name for the girls.

"Grandfather!" they cheered in chorus and hung to his neck.

"Wait till we tell you…." Henrietta started.

"You won't believe…." Rachel Lee interrupted.

"Tell him about Mr. Crane at…." Henrietta started

again.

"Hold it...hold it!" Dr. MacNeil interrupted as he threw his hands in the air. "One at a time," he mused. "Get your grandmother's vanity stool and come over here and tell me all about it," he enthusiastically instructed.

The girls retrieved the stool, and placed it beside their grandfather.

"Rachel Lee, tell him about meeting Mr. Crane," Henrietta encouraged, "you saw him first...and he talked to you."

Rachel Lee eagerly launched into her story. Dr. MacNeil listened intently. She related their meeting at the corral and their run-in with him on upper Central Avenue a few minutes later. Then she ended with a question. "Do you think he's written a story?" Rachel Lee assumed everyone had heard of her grandfather and didn't think it was unusual that a stranger might have written a story for him. "After all," Rachel Lee thought proudly to herself, "Grandfather is a well-known fever specialist, and has written on different kinds of fevers, and been published in medical journals."

"Well, I don't think he's written a story for me personally," he assured her.

"Have you ever met him?" Henrietta asked.

"Well, yes, twice actually, but only once in person," he teased. The girls looked puzzled. "We met first through letters," Dr. MacNeil said, explaining his riddle.

"Oh!" the girls chimed.

Dr. MacNeil knew he couldn't leave it at that, so he explained his relationship with the young newspaperman from New York. "A while back," he started, "Mr. Crane sent a telegram to Dr. Moore and me in care of the drug store. The young man said he had started writing a story about the war."

Their grandfather thought a moment before he continued. "He didn't want to write about the glory of it, but about one man's experience, his struggle with all the horrible things a soldier has to endure in war."

Rachel Lee and Henrietta knew how their grandfather felt about the war. He called it a collective insanity. He said the whole country had gone mad like a raccoon with rabies.

"He didn't want to write about the officers who planned and executed the war, but about the soldiers who had to fight the battles. He wanted to know how all the awfulness of it affected them, and how it changed their lives."

The girls were aware that their grandfather and his friend Dr. R. H. Moore had seen most of the awfulness of war, and they knew a lot about how it had affected the soldiers—and their grandmother, too, she had nursed many soldiers.

Their grandfather's eyes knitted into a frown of sad remembrance. "The men who were drafted," he continued, "on both sides...drafted by talk of honor and promises of glory—that's who he wanted to write about." The frown vanished as quickly as it had

101

appeared. "It was called, *Private Fleming His Various Battles*," he stated with forced cheerfulness. "R. H. was still coroner then and too busy to write. But we did discuss several of our cases," he explained, "those we treated during and after the war in Virginia, and then here in Arkansas. Mr. Crane and I ended up writing to each other quite a bit," he concluded.

"How did he find you?" Rachel Lee asked, always wanting to know the how and why of things.

"Well, it's the funniest thing," Dr. MacNeil answered. "He found our parole papers in some official documents in the nation's capital. Can you imagine that?"

The girls didn't think it was unusual that their grandfather's name was on a piece of paper in Washington D. C., but they were not at all sure what a parole paper was.

"What's a parole paper?" Henrietta asked before Rachel Lee could.

"Remember how your grandmother and I met," he started.

The girls nodded yes.

It was one of Rachel Lee's favorite stories. After graduating from medical school in 1861 their grandfather and Dr. Moore were mustered into the Confederate Army and attached to the 17th Mississippi infantry. They fought at the battle of Spotsylvania, Virginia, and then were captured and held prisoner. That's when her grandparents met. She was helping to nurse the soldiers at the Confederate hospital.

"Well," he continued, "Dr. Moore and I were asked by the Union officers to help some of their soldiers, and I guess somewhere there are records of our service to the Union soldiers," he stated. "That delayed our move out west. But of course as you know, we ended up staying in Virginia even longer than we intended because of the "Great Epizootic" of 1872. We did a lot of walking in those days…if we had only left the year before," he concluded.

Rachel Lee had heard talk about the Great Epizootic all her life. She still found it hard to imagine that millions of horses all got sick in less than five months, or what it must have been like not to have horses to pull the wagons, trolleys, fire trucks and canal boats.

"But how did he know you were in Hot Springs, Arkansas?" Rachel Lee asked.

"Well, that's easy honey!" he exclaimed. "He's a newspaperman. It's his business to know how to find things out, but my guess is he looked me up in *Polk's Medical Registry*. I've been in it now for the past few years. It's a big book with names of all the doctors in the country. It tells what kind of doctor they are, if they went to medical school, where they went to school, and where they now practice," he explained.

"So, what is a parole paper?" Henrietta asked again, as curious as Rachel Lee.

"Oh yes, the parole paper," he responded. "Well it was toward the end of the war and all us soldiers…on both sides… just wanted to go home. The Union boys were glad to let us go because they didn't want to be responsible for us. So they had us sign a piece of paper, called a parole paper, saying we could go home if we promised not to do any more fighting." Dr. MacNeil sat up straighter in his chair, reshuffled his position and continued. "Well, R. H. and I stayed in the area for a few years, tending to veterans from both sides. Right when we were set to head west the Epizootic hit and there wasn't a healthy horse to be found anywhere, so we spent a good deal more time with the veterans. Guess young Mr. Crane figured by our experience that we knew plenty about how the war affected the men who fought it."

"You said you met Mr. Crane twice," Rachel Lee reminded her grandfather.

"Yeah," Henrietta agreed.

"Actually, he left only a short time ago," their grandfather announced.

"He was here?" Rachel Lee asked in surprise.

"Yes," Dr. MacNeil confirmed.

"Oh pooh," Rachel Lee declared her dis-appointment.

"He was sorry to miss you girls as well, but he had to catch the train to New Orleans. By the way," he continued, "he did leave me a copy of a story he is working on. The one he called *Private Fleming His Various Battles*. It's over there," and he pointed across the room to a small writing desk. "Could you get it for me honey?" he asked Henrietta.

Henrietta retrieved a tattered stack of large papers bound with a side ribbon. "This is funny paper," she said, handing the papers to her grandfather.

"It's called 'foolscap'," he instructed, "lawyers use it. He probably doesn't have enough money to write on regular stationary," he concluded. "It's the same story he was working on, but he changed the title." Dr. MacNeil folded over the first protective cover sheet and turned the manuscript around, so the girls could see the title page.

The girls read the title aloud, "*The Red Badge of Courage*, by Stephen Crane."

"He wanted me to have a copy to look over, and see if I had any other suggestions before it went to print. Said I helped him out a lot...gave him some good insight."

"That was swell of him," Rachel Lee declared.

"Indeed it was," Dr. MacNeil replied as he laid the manuscript on top of the almanac beside his chair. "It's going to be interesting to see what he has written. Now," he continued, "tell me what else you girls have on your plate?" he implored.

"I guess Grandmother told you about the fancy Scotsman," Henrietta chimed.

"Yes!" he laughed at her description. "Now there's a puzzle. I can't even," he raised his eyebrows and stretched out the word, "imagine why someone from Edinburgh, Scotland would want to see me," he stated.

"I think he's going to give you something also," Henrietta offered.

"Well," he responded, "we will all know tomorrow. He's supposed to drop by late in the afternoon."

"That's what we heard," Henrietta acknowledged, "but I bet you don't know about the man in the wheelchair."

"I give up," her grandfather gleefully played along, "what wheelchair man?"

"Henry told us about him," Henrietta started, and then continued to tell the incident between Henry, Mr. Johnson, and the wheelchair man.

When she had finished their grandfather thought a moment and then stated, "How very intriguing, and you say he has something for me also?" he asked.

Henrietta nodded yes.

"I'm not sure I want to stick around," he joked. "What do they say—be wary of strangers bearing gifts!"

The girls giggled loudly.

"What's all this levity in here?" their grandmother called out from the bedroom door.

"Levity, what is that?" Rachel Lee asked inquisitively.

"Means we're having fun and being silly," Dr. MacNeil laughed.

Rachel Lee admired her Grandmother's gift with words. She didn't know how in the world she was going to learn all of them, but she knew she was going to try.

Annie crossed the room to stand beside her husband and placed a hand on his shoulder. "Honey," she addressed the love of her life, "I think someone needs to get dressed."

"Yes, dear!" he mocked in meek obedience.

Chapter 13

Wheelchair Man Comes To Call

Everyone welcomed Annie's Sunday dinner of chicken pot pie. Leftover dessert pie from the night before was also a treat.

It was also the only day of the week Mary wasn't around to help out, so the girls and their grandmother had extra kitchen duties. The whole household routine changed on Sundays. Invalid boarders did not go for their baths, church caused a delay in dinner as well as supper, and everyone was pretty much on their own for most of the afternoon.

"Oh pooh, I missed again," Henrietta cried out in frustration.

Spread out on the west window seat of their bedroom, the girls played jacks, as they watched out for the Scotsman and wheelchair man. They had a good view since their house faced Prospect Avenue, and they knew any visitors, not from the Market Street Plaza neighborhood, would probably arrive from that direction.

Their grandparents and Samuel were downstairs in the parlor catching up on the week. The girls promised to let them know when they spotted the arrival of a visitor.

"Looks like the leaves are about to show on the mountain," Henrietta stated as she looked out the window.

From their vantage point the girls had a view of West Mountain and Prospect Avenue almost down to the Baptist church, a block away, where Quapaw Avenue forks into Prospect.

"You want me to look so I'll miss," Rachel Lee accused her cousin and swept up a handful of jacks.

They had played several hands, and had worked up to around the world. Rachel Lee was ahead, but barely.

"The wheelchair man is going to be first...here he comes!" Henrietta shouted.

Rachel Lee stopped her ball before it bounced, leaned around, and peered down at the street at the very moment that the carriage halted.

While Rachel Lee peered out, Henrietta raced for the door. A second later Rachel Lee jumped from her seat and followed her cousin down the stairs two at a time.

"The wheelchair man is here!" Henrietta shouted to her grandparents.

"Heaven sakes, child," her grandmother scolded, "don't let him hear you."

Her father frowned.

"I'm sorry," she lowered her voice.

Samuel stood up. "I'll let him in," he offered

"You girls stay here," he commanded.

They obeyed and decided to make themselves at home on the couch.

A moment later there was a knock on the door. Uncle Samuel greeted the wheelchair man and his helper.

As the visitors entered the family parlor the MacNeils stood.

"Father," Samuel announced, "this is Mr. Lawrence Sawyer from Ohio and his aide Benjamin Tillman."

Dr. MacNeil shook the man's hand. "Please, come in," he addressed his visitors. "Have a seat," he offered Benjamin.

"You don't remember me," Mr. Sawyer, stated in a serious tone.

Dr. MacNeil took a long look at the man in the wheelchair, but saw nothing familiar about him.

Everyone noticed the package on his lap.

"Perhaps this will make things clear." Mr. Sawyer stated as he picked up his package. The smile on his face showed he was pleased with his surprise. "Benjamin," he instructed his aide. "Please hand this to Dr. MacNeil."

Mr. Tillman retrieved the package, regarding it with great care as if it were a treasure of importance, and handed it over to Dr. MacNeil.

"I've waited thirty years to give this back to you," he asserted.

"Give it back!" Dr. MacNeil responded in surprise.

The package was soft to his touch. Carefully he untied the ribbon surrounding the object, and pulled back the wrapping to expose a large grey winter coat. The veteran surgeon of the great American Civil War gasped in utter astonishment.

Rachel Lee watched her speechless grandfather unsuccessfully blink back a gush of tears, as he peered at the gentleman caller and back at the object in his lap.

"My coat!" he choked, his whole body radiating from the pain of a tortured past.

"You remember," Mr. Sawyer spoke softly.

Everyone in the room was silent. Rachel Lee could hear the muffled sound of a carriage passing by, and the penetrating tic-toc of the grandfather's clock. Her grandmother displayed a deep sadness in her expression.

A little apprehensive, Henrietta instinctively moved closer to her cousin. The girls had never seen their grandfather so emotional.

Dr. MacNeil looked at the legless man in the wheelchair. "I had to do it," he spoke and swallowed hard.

"I know," Mr. Sawyer assured him.

Dr. MacNeil started to say something and then tried again, but all he could do was swallow hard and blink back tears.

Mr. Sawyer looked up and addressed Samuel, who was standing to one side of the fireplace. "Your father saved my life," he stated simply and then told the story. "It was early spring and cold, like now, and I was separated from my company. My legs were useless...all torn up. I managed to drag myself up to the roadway and propped myself up against a tree."

Rachel Lee knew from years of hearing her grandparents and other adults in the community talk of the war that this was a story Mr. Sawyer had repeated many times before.

He hesitated for a moment and then continued. "I don't remember how long I was there, but it seemed like forever. After a time I passed out and the next thing I knew," his voice changed to a lighter tone, "something jarred me back into consciousness, and there staring at me was that big old rebel coat," he ended with an uplift of humor.

A small chuckle escaped from both her grandparents. The tension broke and uncertainty shattered. Dr. MacNeil took up the story.

"And it was a good thing you passed out again," Dr. MacNeil explained, once again in control of himself.

"Those were terrible times," he addressed the whole room, and then turned to his fellow veteran. "I did the best I could. I didn't know if you would make it or not...chances were you would not." He looked down at his coat then back up at Mr. Sawyer. "But I knew you had to stay warm if you were going to have a chance at all," he ended.

Again, there was a momentary silence broken by the soft gentle voice of Rachel Lee's grandmother.

"How in the world did you survive, and what made you bring the coat now?" she inquired.

Mr. Sawyer talked about his recovery. "Normally your coat would have been tossed aside when they took me back to camp, but blankets were in short supply." He took a deep breath before continuing. "I had regained enough strength to guard it by the time they transported me back up north. No one questioned why I had the coat. They all thought I simply wanted a rebel trophy. After the war…" he hesitated, "well it took me a long, long time before I recovered enough to make inquiries into your whereabouts. I tried for a while and then gave up hope."

For a moment there was silence, and then Dr. MacNeil spoke. "I think there was chaos everywhere after the war. Then the *Great Epizootic* happened, and so many horses and mules died that it was a long time before we could migrate."

We moved from Virginia in 1878, and joined others in the move out west," Annie offered.

"Settled in the village of Cedar Glades west of here till '88, and then decided to move in to Hot Springs," Dr. MacNeil further explained.

Her grandparents and Mr. Sawyer talked of things past for a while longer, and then her grandmother offered refreshments which Mr. Sawyer declined. "I appreciate your hospitality, but we must be going," he begged off. "Maybe I'll be back this way one of these days."

"You are welcome in our home anytime," Rachel Lee's grandmother graciously offered.

"Anytime!" her grandfather echoed.

After Mr. Sawyer left, Mrs. MacNeil took charge of the routine. "Girls, it's about time we get supper started," she declared, and marshaled the cousins in the direction of the kitchen, leaving Samuel and his father on their own in the parlor.

ର୍ଭର୍ଭର୍ଭର୍ଭର୍ଭର୍ଭର୍ଭର୍ଭର୍ଭର୍ଭର୍ଭର୍ଭର୍ଭର୍ଭ

Chapter 14

Scotsman Comes to Call

"But what about the Scotsman?" Henrietta whined.

"What about him," Mrs. MacNeil responded to her granddaughter as they entered the kitchen.

"Well, shouldn't we be on the lookout for him?" Henrietta explained, still whining.

"That would be nice, honey," she answered, an edge creeping into her voice, "but it's getting late, and the supper hour is going to be on us before we know it. Besides, I think if that Scotsman could find his way here all the way from Edinburgh, Scotland, he can find our house."

Henrietta and Rachel Lee were both crestfallen.

"But…," Rachel Lee started. It was her time to whine.

"Girls, please don't whine!" Mrs. MacNeil pleaded.

If there was one thing their grandmother could not abide, it was whining.

"But…," Rachel Lee tried again.

"No buts!" her grandmother sharply interrupted. "Now go get me some firewood and water," she ordered.

"Firewood and water," Rachel Lee complained to herself. "That's all there is to my life, firewood and water!"

"Girls," Mrs. MacNeil spoke gently. "If we hurry," she relented, "we can get the beef and barley vegetable soup on, and return to the parlor while it cooks."

That was all the encouragement they needed. In a flash they were out the door to gather firewood, and were back before their grandmother could return from the root cellar.

"Heaven sakes, never seen you two move so fast," their grandmother joked as she poured an armload of cabbage and carrots into the kitchen sink.

For the next few minutes the MacNeil women cut and chopped their way toward supper. The girls talked to their grandmother about their grandfather's experience with Mr. Sawyer, and speculated on what the Scotsman, Bruce McPherson, had to offer.

"Whatever it is," Mrs. MacNeil declared while shaving the sides of a left over-roast. "I hope it's not too big of a surprise. I don't think your grandfather can take another jolt this evening."

A few minutes later the girls were cleaning up their mess when Henrietta heard her father at the front door. "The Scotsman's here!" she cried out.

"Can we clean later?" Rachel Lee begged her grandmother.

"Yes, of course you can," she responded, "but let's clean our hands before we meet our guest," she strongly suggested.

The Scotsman was seated, but stood up along with the MacNeil gentlemen when Mrs. MacNeil and her granddaughters entered.

On introduction, he bowed very formally to Mrs. MacNeil and both girls. Annie returned an equally formal bow. The kind of bow that takes place at the waist, more of a leaning forward, head upright, and slightly tilted in one direction or the other.

Rachel Lee took note and thought, "Grandmother is like that. She could bend with the times, as she liked to say, but she would never sacrifice her good manners, nor would she let her granddaughters grow up without manners."

But Annie's reaction to Mr. McPherson was about more than good manners. Rachel Lee understood her grandmother's polite stiffness in the presence of formal or important people, or those who thought they were important. Her grandmother's polite stiffness reminded her of an oft repeated lesson that both her grandparents adhered too: "*Never stick your nose up in the air to anyone, and never bow your head to anyone but God.*" She knew her grandmother was making that point right now.

The girls took their cue from their grandmother and greeted their guest with the same formality established by the Scotsman.

After they exchanged names and were seated, the Scotsman, Mr. McPherson, spoke, "I'm so glad you could join us," he addressed Mrs. MacNeil, "since this will affect the whole family." He looked from Annie to Dr. MacNeil, leaned to the side, and picked up his writing case. "As I was about to tell your husband," he started, "I am here on official business."

For the next few minutes Mr. McPherson from Edinburgh, Scotland, turned his attention entirely on Dr. MacNeil. He asked him a number of questions about his father's relatives back in Scotland. Then he showed him some official-looking documents, and stated that a distant cousin had died and left his entire estate to his nearest relative.

While Mr. McPherson laid out his most fantastic offer, the cousins looked in each other's direction and silently communicated their lack of a clear understanding for what he was saying.

"As it turns out, Dr. MacNeil, you are Lord MacNeil's closest relative. You would inherit much more than a title, though," Mr. McPherson explained, "there is land, a castle, and of course…"

The girls shot each other a look of great delight. They didn't hear a thing after *castle*. They were going to live in Scotland, in a castle!

Sometime later, Mr. McPherson concluded his business with the MacNeils, said he knew this was a big decision, and would get back in touch with them in the near future.

"A castle," Rachel Lee spoke in hushed excitement to her cousin. "Imagine that, we're going to live in a castle."

"So all Grandfather has to do is go live in Scotland, and he will get land, a title and a castle?" she asked.

"I think so, that's what it sounds like to me," she answered.

Chapter 15

Mr. in America

The girls couldn't stop chattering. They talked in the kitchen, at the supper table, and then back in the kitchen to clean up after supper.

"We'll have servants, and we'll never have to do dishes again," Henrietta happily chirped.

"No more fetching wood and water," Rachel Lee cheered.

"Hurray!" they exclaimed.

Neither girl had noticed that their grandparents and Samuel had said very little since the Scotsman departed.

With the dishes finished, and the kitchen cleaned and readied for the next morning, their grandparents broke their silence. "Girls," their grandmother addressed them on entering the kitchen, "I need you to come into the parlor. Your grandfather would like to have a word with you."

The girls' excitement level soared. Their grandfather had already thought it over and made up his mind, they were going to Scotland to live.

They hurried to the parlor, eager for their grandfather to tell them the news. They returned to the couch, and their grandmother settled in her usual chair.

"It's hard not to notice your excitement about the prospect of moving to Scotland," their grandfather began. There was lightness to his voice, and then he spoke more seriously. "But I cannot accept Mr. McPherson's offer," he stated flatly.

Rachel Lee's life turned upside down for the second time in one evening. "Why?" Rachel Lee responded in disbelief. She didn't understand.

"He said you could think about it," Henrietta moaned.

Their grandfather, who had been sitting on the edge of his chair, leaned back and sighed. For all that life had handed him he still remembered what it was like to be young and full of dreams and fantasies. He hated to disappoint them, but it was a relief to break the news to the girls. Life handed everyone disappointments and he never wanted to add to theirs.

"Henrietta, honey," he affectionately explained, "I don't need to think about it." Smiling he continued, "I only told the dear man I would think about it, because I didn't want him to feel rejected so quickly, after he had traveled so far and gone to such trouble to find me."

"But why, grandfather?" Rachel Lee fought back her disappointment.

Her grandfather leaned his head back against his overstuffed sofa chair, an expression of thought on his face. Then he rolled his head over toward his wife, and Rachel Lee watched a knowing smile slide across her face. Then he looked toward the fireplace, and for a moment he watched the flames dance. When he started to talk, his voice was rich and mellow, and he spoke of many important things. Mostly, though, he talked of a love etched deep in his soul, a love of his country, of the idea of equality. His words were of one man's struggle against the torrents and tides of his time, and all mankind's struggle to be free.

When he spoke his voice was soft, almost a whisper, as though he were talking out loud to himself. "President Jefferson wrote, *Man was not born with a saddle on his back, to be ridden by the booted and privileged few.*"

"Do you understand?" he gently asked.

The girls nodded that they did, even though they were not entirely sure they understood.

Their grandfather sat up straight and appeared to shake off life's burdens before he addressed them again. "Let me put it this way," he spoke almost boisterously. "I'd rather be called Mr. in America than King anywhere else in the world, and some day you are going to feel the same way."

Chapter 16

Final Thought of the Day

Rachel Lee lay awake long after she and Henrietta and the rest of the family had retired for the evening. So much had happened in the past two days.

"Three mysteries solved in two days. It would be more than a body could take if this much excitement happened every day," she thought to herself.

A storm had developed early in the evening at sunset, and the wind and rain clamored at the windows, and swirled around the belfry. The rain that fell on the tin roof above vibrated in soothing rhythmic tones.

"I can't believe Henrietta and I thought for even a moment of leaving Hot Springs. What were we thinking?" Rachel Lee chided herself. "Besides, having too much has its own problems," as she had often observed, "and I can't imagine life without Henry and Jake, Max, Mary, and everyone else. I wasn't thinking," she concluded. "I guess we had a touch of what Grandfather calls mass hysteria."

She also knew she didn't have to wait for someday when it came to the question of being called Miss in America, or Queen anywhere else in the world.

For a long time she stared at the trap door in the ceiling, and listened as the bell softly chimed against the storm. In time she drifted off to sleep, comforted by the bell's soft refrain—her family's very own liberty bell.

She and those she cared for were safe and warm, held securely in the strong arms of her country's freedom, and her family's love. In this certain knowledge she dreamed of things past and present, and as for the future, with all its mysteries, well, she left those for another day.

Annie MacNeil's Chicken Pot Pie Recipe

3 cups cooked chicken
1 cup carrots
1 cup onions
1 cup celery
1 cup cooked green peas
2 cups chicken stock
2 cups milk
½ cup flour
1 teaspoon Worcestershire sauce
1 teaspoon salt
Pinch of: rosemary, thyme, sage, marjoram, black
pepper and nutmeg. (or) [1 tbsp poultry seasoning]

Egg wash
1 egg
2 teaspoon water

Boil chicken until done. Save stock. Cook carrots,
onions and celery in 2 cups chicken stock for 10 to 15
minutes. Drain vegetables and set aside.

Over medium heat place drained chicken stock (2
cups) into large pot along with Worcestershire sauce,
salt, herbs [poultry seasoning] and stir.

Whisk in flour for 1 to 2 minutes. Reduce heat to low,
pour in milk and simmer for 5 minutes. Add

vegetables. Simmer for 5 minutes more. Stir occasionally.
Heat oven to 400°

Prepare pie crust dough. (or) [2 (9-inch) pie crusts]

Line large baking bowl with dough. Cook for 7 minutes at 400°

Place warm filling in bowl and cover with rest of dough, brush with egg wash, and cut 3 inch slit in top. Bake for at least 45 minutes or until filling bubbles and crust is golden brown.

Cool 10 minutes before serving.

Serves 8 to 10.

GLOSSARY OF TERMS

Bazaar – In Eastern countries a market or street of shops.

Belfry – The part of a tower or steeple that holds a bell.

Capitalist – Owner of wealth used in business.

Confectionery Shop – Candy store.

Dispensary – A place were medicines and medical treatment are given free or for a small fee.

Emporium – A large store with a wide variety of things for sale.

Indigent – Poor person.

Legal foolscap – A kind of writing paper, varying in size from 8 ½ by 14 inches to13 by 16 inches, with the fold at the top and used by lawyers.

Levity – Lightness or gaiety of disposition.

Moors – Arab and Berber inhabitants of northwestern Africa.

Privy House – A small shelter outside a house containing a toilet.

Q. T. – (*slang*) In secret.

Rheumatism and/or Rheumatic Fever – Used in colloquial speech and historical contexts. Non-specific term for medical problems that cause fever, pain and swelling of the joints and muscles, inflammation of the heart valves; affects heart, bones, joints, kidney, skin and lungs.

Salubrious - Healthful.

Tarpaulin - Waterproofed canvas.

Towhead – Pale-yellow hair

City Business Directory

Selected Businesses from 1897 Hot Springs, Arkansas

—**Adams Robert H,** hack driver, Worthington, bds Alton House

—**Alhambra Bathhouse,** 114 Ouachita ave

—**Arkansas National Bank,** 428 Central ave

— **Arlington Hotel,** Central cor Fountain

—**Carver A Mrs,** confectr, 194 Central ave

—**Cutter Charles,** editor Hot Springs Illustrated Journal, 515 Central ave

— **Great Northern Hotel,** 1Benton

— **Graves John C, hides, etc,** rear 102 Ouachita ave

—**McDonald Meat Market,** 205 Market Street

—**Moore Milton P,** druggist 102 Ouachita ave, furms 107 Ouachita ave., res same

—**Moore Mrs RH, boarding house, 215 Prospect ave.**

—**Moore Robert H,** phys 102 Ouachita ave, res 215 Prospect

—**Plateau Hotel,** 736 Central ave

— **Rozzetti M Mrs,** confectr, 168 Central ave

—**Taylor Carlton F (Taylor & Moore),** res 613 Orange

—**Taylor Daniel T,** phys 638 1/2 Central ave, res 613 Orange

—**Taylor & Moore Drug Store,** 102 Ouachita ave

—**Tennessee Wagon Yard,** 211 Market

— **Turf Exchange,** 328 Central ave

—**Worthington, Lee,** mine owner, bds Great Northern hotel

1897 Hot Springs City Business Directory
Courtesy of: *Arkansas Historical Commission*